'The studio.'
to get into t.

'Maybe it'

Just then tl
breaking glass
Slow down, he

We both jum_ ... we heard more
crashing and thumping – this time more
frantic. Whatever they were after, they
were desperate.

Machine-gun heart, crumbly bones,
clammy forehead – my whole human
system was breaking down. Any second
now and I'd be a gibbering idiot.

Then the thumping stopped.

There was a different sound.

A soft, sly, hissing sound.

An eerily familiar sound ... I
remembered then where I'd heard that
sound before ...

Also by Mary Arrigan:
DEAD MONKS AND SHADY DEALS
LANDSCAPE WITH CRACKED SHEEP
SEASCAPE WITH BARBER'S HARP

Mary Arrigan

THE SPIRITS OF THE BOG

THE CHILDREN'S PRESS

First published 1998 by
The Children's Press
an imprint of Anvil Books
45 Palmerston Road, Dublin 6

2 4 6 5 3 1

ISBN 1 901737 10 1

Cover illustration Jonathan Barry
Cover design Terry Myler
Typeset by Computertype Limited
Printed by Colour Books Limited

To Bennie

1

It was kind of lonesome watching the bus disappear down the country road. It was like watching the whole world moving away leaving me totally alone, like in those sci-fi films where everyone gets nuked except for some nervous individual left to watch out for any alien types who might be mooching about. I like films like that. They're fine when you're sprawled on your own sofa in your own living-room munching crisps with a couple of mates, but you don't want to be imagining stuff like that when you're about to shuffle down a winding lane through a load of trees.

Mum says that Grandma Kate is a nutter. 'Why she wants to be stuck out there in the bog, miles from civilisation, I just don't know,' she'd say to Dad. 'Your mother is totally weird.'

Dad would just smile and nod. 'Kate is herself,' he'd reply. Which, in itself is a pretty weird thing to say. How can you be someone else's self?

I'd never come to Grandma Kate's on my own before, and certainly not by bus. I glanced back to catch a last glimpse of it, but there was just a puff of dust over the hill. I was now really alone. I picked up my rucksack and headed towards the narrow lane that led through the trees. I'd never noticed the sound of trees before. Even on a day like this, with no wind and a sun that made it even too hot for bees to buzz, they rustled their branches and made sighing noises.

I'm not by nature a wimpy type. I don't scare easily, but I kind of wished that Grandma Kate had come to meet me at the top of the lane. Then I realised I was being a total nerd, so I banished all stupid thoughts of stupid aliens in stupid films and whistled as loudly as I could. Completely out of tune, of course, but a darn sight nicer to listen to than those crummy trees.

I had just rounded the last bend before Grandma Kate's cottage when I felt the first shiver. You know how it is when you've been in the hot sun and you suddenly open the fridge door to get a drink. Well, it was like that – only there was no fridge door; I was still in the sunlight, but I was freezing. I was so amazed I stepped back and felt the hot sun again. Then I went forward and was immediately touched by an icy cold that made me shiver again.

Now I knew I was being a total nerd. 'Trick of the weather,' I told myself. 'Hot weather can do weird things.'

I thought about really hot deserts where people sometimes imagine a cool oasis ahead and fall flat on their noses in the sand. Common sense took over and I forged ahead.

'Hey!' a cry rang out. In the clearing ahead, Grandma Kate's cottage nestled in its overgrown garden – Grandma Kate just liked to have wild flowers in her garden. She wasn't one for garden centres and fancy roses.

'Hey!' the cry rang out again and someone was waving from the low branches of a chestnut-tree.

I forgot about the shivery bit when I realised who was shouting and waving.

2

'I didn't know you were going to be here too,' I said, looking up into the branches.

My cousin, Susy, leapt down and stood before me, her hands on her hips. She's trouble with a capital T. Nearly eleven years old, she's five months younger than me and miles shorter. With her skinny, stick-insect body and big red hair, she's like a flaming match.

'And if I'd known *you* were coming, Arty Adams, I'd have stowed away on a ship to the Outer Headbrides,' she retorted, nodding her head and making her springy curls wobble.

'*Hebrides*,' I scoffed.

'What?'

'The word is Hebrides,' I said. 'The Outer Hebrides. And I for one wish you *had* stowed away on a ship to there.'

'Huh,' she said.

'Huh,' I said. Great start. Now, more than ever I wished I hadn't let that bus out of my sight. The thoughts of being stuck here with her and a load of rustling trees for company did nothing for my well-being.

Susy gave a mean laugh and pointed to my feet. 'I see you're still wearing cheapo canvas boots,' she said.

'So what?' I snapped. The canvas boots had caused major grief between my mum and me; I had wanted something a bit more classy. Something with gel insets and flashing lights, you know the sort of trainers I mean – mega bucks and mega attitude. But Mum had insisted on these insignificant canvas things.

'These are nice and light on your feet for the summer,' she'd said.

'Nice and light on your purse, you mean,' I'd complained.

'That too,' admitted Mum. 'No point in shelling out vast sums on something you'll grow out of in a few weeks. Or have them stolen on you. You won't have to worry about these being stolen.'

'Stolen!' I'd said. 'Mum, I'd have to pay someone to nick these.'

Mum had just laughed.

Susy held out one foot. It was encased in just the sort of footwear I'd wanted. Seriously trendy trainers.

'Get a load of these,' she said. 'Eighty quid's worth. Now these are real trainers. Like having Rolls Royce cars on your feet.'

I wanted to say something really meaning-ful and rude about her feet and her fancy trainers, but I couldn't think of anything to say, I was that peeved.

'Arty!' Grandma Kate's voice cut across our battle front. She swept down the path and smothered me in a hug. She smelled of turpentine and there were paint stains on her smock and jeans. Her hair had once been the colour of Susy's, but now it was kind of streaky and tied back in a ponytail. She's not thin, but she's not what you'd call fat either. She's a sort of a comfy shape.

'Did you travel on the bus all on your own? I meant to be there to meet you, but you know me – time kind of gets lost around here. See, your cousin Susy's here too.'

Susy made a face at me over Grandma Kate's shoulder.

'Will you talk to the hedgehog?' she went on, wiping the paint she'd smeared on my sweat shirt and making it worse. 'Susy has tried, but the little beggar won't stay quiet for her.'

That's the great thing about Grandma Kate; she never says boring things like 'How are you getting on at school?' or 'My, how big you've grown.' She's at ease and off-beat with everyone. She's a smashing artist. Not just a Sunday painter of watery flowers and sunsets on sticky seas, but one of the best wild-life painters in the country. Her pictures are on calendars, Christmas cards and in picture books. So you can see why her house, which is beside the forest and a bog, is just right for all that sort of stuff.

'Why is *she* here?' I asked. I know, I know – a tad on the sullen side, but there was a whole holiday at stake here.

'Because I want her here,' said Grandma Kate. 'You are both my grandchildren and I like having my grandchildren to stay. Now come on, let's see about this hedgehog.'

I followed her into the cool, tiled hallway of her cottage, rubbing the paint stain on my sweat shirt and noticing that now I too was smelling of turps.

Grandma Kate's studio is really a big glasshouse off the kitchen. Unlike some picky painters, Grandma Kate likes lots of light. She says it gives her pictures their vivid colouring. The hedgehog had fallen asleep on a bed of leaves on the paint-spattered table, a cloth draped like a canopy above him to keep the sunlight off. Grandma Kate's half-finished picture stood on an easel. She gestured.

'Meet Hoggy. Portrait of a hedgehog.'

'That's super,' I said. 'Really cool.'

Grandma Kate smiled. 'You do my old heart good, Arty,' she said. 'I know if you like it that the rest of the world will like it too.'

Susie was miffed. 'Yeah,' she said. 'But why

all the fuss about a *live* hedgehog? If you go out on the road you'll find loads of squashed ones. Then you wouldn't have to worry about it moving around.'

I glanced at Grandma Kate to see if she was shocked, but I should have known better. Nothing the outrageous Susy says ever annoys her. 'Flat hedgehogs don't make very nice pictures,' she said.

'Live ones are fat and they smell,' retorted Susy.

'Like you,' I said, delighted to get a jibe at Miss Trouble.

'Cool it, you two,' said Grandma Kate, rinsing her brush in a jam jar and wiping it on a rag. 'Bickering makes bad vibes and I don't want bad vibes in my house.' She wrapped a cloth around the hedgehog and picked him up.

'Here, little fellow,' she said. 'I've enough of your lovely mush to go on with. Out you go, back to your prickly mammy.' She opened the glass door and gently put him in the long grass. He sniffed and dithered for a moment and scurried into the undergrowth. Grandma Kate laughed and turned back towards us.

'Come over here,' she said, crossing over to the rack where she kept big sketchbooks and canvases. 'Let me show you the drawings for my next picture.' She pulled out the biggest sketchbook and turned back the cover. As she did so, a cloud passed over the sun and a sudden chill seemed to invade the studio. I shivered with that same fridge-door shiver that I'd got earlier in the forest.

I gasped when I saw the drawing that Grandma Kate was holding up. It was not like any other picture she had ever done. It was an old, gnarled tree rising out of the boggy peatland. Its massive roots were exposed like thick, grasping fingers. She had drawn every whorl and split on its rough bark. It was terrifyingly alive. I didn't like it. Not one little bit.

'Wow! That's dead brill, Grandma Kate,' said Susy. 'It's like ... it's like it's reaching out to grab you.'

Grandma Kate smiled. 'Arty?' she said, looking at me for my reaction. I swallowed hard, wondering how I'd get out of this without hurting her feelings.

'It's different,' I said, marvelling at my quick cleverness. 'Very different.'

She laughed. 'It's certainly that,' she said. 'Come on, let's have a bite to eat. I've made a gooey chocolate cake just for you.'

She closed the sketchbook and, as she did so, the cloud passed from in front of the sun and the studio lost that awful chill.

3

'You can both come with me to the bog,' Grandma Kate said as we wiped the last of the chocolate off our fingers. 'I want to continue with that sketch of the tree.'

'Good, I'll make some sketches too,' said Susy. 'I want to be an artist when I grow up. But not hedgehogs and bunnies and daisies and that kind of stuff. I want to be a scary, horror artist.'

How could I resist an opening like that? 'You already are a scary horror,' I said. 'Not much more you'd have to learn about that, is there?'

Susy's face turned into a squashed cherry, all red and wrinkled. She started to say something but Grandma Kate cut in.

'Cool it,' she said, taking her battered straw hat from a nail behind the kitchen door. 'Come on, before the light begins to fade.'

We took the grassy path that led through the forest to the bog. Our feet made squishy sounds on the long grass. The trees still rustled, but that didn't matter now that there were three of us. Except it made me realise all the more what a nerd I'd been earlier on to be spooked by them.

We came to the part of the bog where Grandma Kate did most of her work. This was a smaller bog surrounded by trees and shrubs. Beyond the trees was the main bog where people spent their summers cutting and bagging turf. You could hear the distant throb of the machines, but all that activity never intruded on this secluded spot. Apart from Grandma Kate, nobody bothered to come here much. She said that the whole ancient spirit of the bog was in this small haven. She called it her secret garden.

'Look at those colours,' she said to Susy and me as we came into the clearing. 'Purple heather, brown peat and green shrubs. And the phlox. Look at those pinks and mauves.'

Susy and I glanced at one another and sniggered. Grandma Kate gets totally hyper about colours. If the world suddenly turned black and white she'd go mental.

'And the woodbine,' she went on. 'Can you smell the woodbine?' She looked at Susy and me and caught us sniggering. She pretended disgust. 'Might have known,' she said. 'You're just a couple of...' She broke off and looked beyond us, frowning.

A man was walking along the perimeter of

the bog. Every now and then he'd stop, pick up a handful of peat and crumble it between his fingers. He was small and thin, with a stoop which made his jacket hang like a cheap curtain over his baggy pants. His black hair was gelled so much it looked like plastic. When he saw us, he wandered over.

'Evening, Ma'am,' he nodded.

Grandma Kate bristled slightly. 'Evening,' she said stiffly. 'Are you admiring the scenery, Mr Kitt?'

The man smiled and shook his head. 'Getting ready to move in the heavy machinery,' he said. 'This place will be a hive of activity next week.'

'So, you're going ahead with this scheme after all?' said Grandma Kate. 'You've made up your mind? In spite of what David Bellamy and the other conservation people have said about this...this unique haven? In spite of the petition that so many of us signed? Doesn't that mean anything to you?'

'You know very well,' the man's smile was replaced by a hostile glare, 'you know I'm going to drain and develop this place for cutaway bog.'

'I know what you're after, young man,' snapped Grandma Kate. 'But your father told me many times that he would never do anything to this piece of bog. He loved it as much as I do. He liked to come here. He was proud of this place, your father.'

Susy and I forgot our sniggering and looked at one another with amazement. We'd never seen our grandma like this before.

'My father is dead,' retorted Mr Kitt. 'I've taken over now and I intend to make the land pay. He left this place idle for years, but I intend selling the turf...'

'You can't do that!' exclaimed Grandma Kate. 'You can't cut big drains like...like scars through this lovely spot. Haven't you any feelings for nature and beauty? What about the wildlife? Your father was content to work the larger bog on the other side of the forest. He made his fortune from that – and you're still making your fortune from it. He said he'd never touch here, that he would leave it to nature.'

Susy moved closer to me. Neither of us said anything, but we felt that we were the troops waiting to go to battle. Any more guff out of this creep and we'd knock him into the swampiest part of the bog.

He was getting angry now. 'Like I just said, Missus,' he snarled, 'I'm in charge now. There's plenty of room in the rest of the countryside for flowers and things. You can paint your pretty pictures there. I'm more interested in people, in giving them turf for their fires. Cheap fuel.'

'You're interested in lining your pockets, you mean,' put in Grandma Kate. 'How much of the land do you need to tear up for that?'

'That's my business,' snapped Mr Kitt. 'Fuel is my business and this,' he gestured towards the the peaceful bog, 'this is part of my business. All you do-gooders ever do is make trouble.'

'Protecting our Irish heritage is trouble?' scoffed Grandma Kate. 'People like you can't see that you're tearing the very soul of the country. If all the natural pockets of wilderness are wiped out, we'll lose more of our native birds and animals and plants. It's no skin off the nose for the likes of you to leave small areas to nature.'

'Look, Missus,' Mr Kitt said with exagger-ated patience, 'you're welcome to come here with your sketchbooks and what-have-you, but don't get in the way of my business. Good day to you.' He strode off towards the track that led to the road on the far side of the bog.

Grandma Kate reached down to restrain Susy who made to run after the retreating figure. 'Let me just give him one kick,' she snarled. 'Just one.'

Grandma Kate laughed and gave the little spitfire a hug. 'Don't waste your good kick,' she said. 'He's just a greedy little upstart. I'll fight the so-and-so to preserve this little bit of heaven. Do you know,' she went on, leading us towards a raised bank, 'that if they were lucky enough in Holland to have a spot like this they'd declare it a national monument? All their bogs were destroyed by years of cutting and draining. And now people like cruddy Kitt are doing the same to ours.'

'Should've let me kick him,' muttered Susy.

'He's not worth the anger,' said Grandma Kate, even though you could see that her hands were still trembling with her own fury. She sighed, took some pencils out of her satchel and opened her big sketchbook. 'A huge chunk of Ireland was once bogland,' she continued. 'Now, because of drainage and cutting it away for turf, and exporting peat abroad as fertiliser, we'll be lucky to have any natural bog by 2015. The plants and wildlife will be extinct. All they're asked to do is leave some.' She gave another great sigh and sat on the bank, propping her sketchbook on her knee. 'Now I'd better get my drawing done – while there's still something to draw.'

Susy was peering over Grandma Kate's shoulder. 'It's different,' she said.

'I said that,' I snorted. 'Back at the studio, I said that. Can't you come up with ...?'

'It's not that,' put in Susy, pointing to the

sketch. 'Look, that tree has moved.'

I snorted again and went to look. The three of us looked at the drawing and then at the tree Grandma Kate had been sketching.

'You're right,' said Grandma Kate. 'It *does* seem to have moved since yesterday's part of the drawing. How odd!'

I felt another one of those fridge-door shivers. I nudged Susy, just so that she'd say something normal to banish that spooky feeling.

'Hey, get off!' she said.

I smiled. That was normal enough for me.

'It looks like it's trying to get out of the bog,' she went on, nodding towards the tree.

'So it does,' mused Grandma Kate. 'There are lots more roots showing now.'

'What does it mean?' I croaked, on account of my throat having suddenly gone dry.

Grandma Kate shrugged and began to sketch. 'I expect it's due to the fine weather we've been having,' she said. 'The ground is probably drying and shrinking. Now, you two amuse yourselves. I want to get this done while there's still sunlight.'

4

But the sun wasn't shining any more. A sort of mist seemed to be rising from the boggy area. A wispy mist that floated about like when you drip some milk into a glass of water.

'Can you give me some paper and the loan of a pencil, Gran?' asked Susy. 'I'd like to sketch that brill tree as well.'

Grandma Kate tore off a half page and handed it to Susy. Susy gave me a smarmy look as much as to say, 'You're too stupid for this kind of thing.'

I scowled and made my way to the edge of the swampy part of the bog. It was like a dark brown lake, except there was no water, just marshy bog. My dad said that sometimes they used to find the bodies of people who'd tried crossing bogs in the old days and got sucked under. Their bodies were preserved by the peat so that, when they were dug up, they looked like they'd just died. I wondered what I'd do if I suddenly saw a body. Might be interesting. Or not. I jumped up and down at the edge and could feel the springy surface shaking.

On the other side, between the wafts of mist, I could see Mr Kitt making his way towards the Land Rover which was parked on the track. I hoped that the wheels would get stuck and he'd ask us for help – which he wouldn't get. I picked up a stick and poked at the marshy surface. I was pretty amazed when a bubble arose and, with a hiss, went down again. No sooner had it sunk than another took its place, and another and another. Soon there were lots of brown bubbles rising and falling with the same hissing sound.

Ssss...ssss... I'd never seen anything like this before. And I didn't much like it. I had a slight touch of freaking out and made my way back to where Grandma Kate and Susy were still sketching. Susy was impatiently scrubbing at her drawing with a rubber.

'I can't do this,' she cried. 'It's stupid.'

'Patience, my dear,' said Grandma Kate, without looking up from her own drawing.

'Patience me eye!' muttered Susy. 'I don't think I want to be an artist after all. I think I'll be an actress instead. Or a long distance lorry driver. This is rubbish.' She screwed up the sketch and threw it towards the marshy bog. No sooner had it touched the surface than it sank with a faint slurp – as if it had been sucked under. In its place dozens of brown bubbles surfaced and hissed.

The fridge-door shiver and dry-throat syndrome hit me again. My mouth opened and shut like a fish on ice. I expect my eyes were bulging too, but I didn't much care how I looked.

'Did you see that?' asked Susy.

I nodded dumbly.

'Mega spooky,' said Susy. 'Did you see that, Grandma Kate?'

'See what?' Grandma Kate was still engrossed in her work.

'The way my sketch...oh, never mind.' Susy went down to the edge of the bog and I followed her, concentrating very heavily on the word *courage*.

'Look at all those mucky bubbles,' went on Susy.

I cleared my throat. 'Listen to them,' I said.

'What?' she looked at me with a puzzled frown.

I nodded towards the bubbles. 'Listen to them.'

'Are you out of your tiny mind...?'

'Just listen,' I insisted.

She closed her mouth and looked again at the brown bubbles. Realisation dawned and she looked at me in amazement. 'Freaky,' she said, giving a slight shiver. It was good to know that she was suffering from the fridge-door thing too. I wasn't all crazy.

Susy glanced back at where Grandma Kate was drawing. 'I hope she's not going to be much longer,' she said. 'I'd sooner be home watching telly.'

I nodded eagerly, like one of those cheapo dogs you see in old cars. For once we were agreed on something.

Ssss...ssss.... The whispering petered out. I looked across to where I'd seen Mr Kitt. Funny, I thought. He should have reached his Land Rover by now. But the Land Rover was still parked and of Mr Kitt there was no sign.

'He must have doubled back into the forest,' I said.

'Who?'

'Kitt. He was heading towards his Land Rover a couple of minutes ago. Now there's no sign of him.'

'I hope he fell into a bog-hole,' snorted Susy.

'Still, pretty weird,' I said.

'This place is doing your pathetic little head in,' laughed Susy. 'He's probably lying in the heather watching to see that we don't run off with his precious bog. Come on. I'm cold. And hungry. And bored. Oh, darn. Look at that.' She bent down and rubbed a peat stain off one of her precious trainers with some spit. 'Dirty old bog,' she said.

We made our way back to Grandma Kate. Her nose was wrinkled and she was shaking her head. 'Botheration,' she said, pointing to the tree she'd been sketching. I nearly lost the power of my knees when I saw that it was almost hidden behind the mist that was now wafting around it.

'I was almost finished,' she went on, ' and now I can't see a thing. The fine weather must be causing the condensation to rise.' She closed the sketchbook and eased herself up stiffly. 'Come on, you two. Time to call it a day.'

'You betcha,' agreed Susy. 'Any crisps, Gran?'

Grandma Kate laughed. 'We'll see what the cupboard has to offer,' she said.

I've made better decisions than the one that prompted me to glance back at that tree. The fridge door opened on to my neck again when I saw that the mist seemed to have split into eerie shapes that wafted around the exposed roots.

5

'Have you not got cable telly yet?' asked Susy.

Grandma Kate shook her head. 'Don't have much call for heavy metal music and massacre films,' she said. Which was a bit extreme, I thought. Two measly channels hardly constitutes half decent entertainment. In some ways perhaps my mum was right. Certain aspects of Grandma Kate's thinking pointed towards the nutter category.

Susy did a lot of sighing as she rifled through the telly page in the newspaper. 'There's a Superman film on in an hour,' she said. 'Probably a repeat.'

'A repeat of a repeat,' I said.

'What'll we do till then?' asked Susy. The desperation in her voice would have given me great satisfaction if I hadn't been wondering the same thing myself. Please God, don't let Grandma Kate suggest Ludo or some ancient game like that. But she had other plans.

'Would you like to see some old pictures?' she asked.

Susy, now sprawled on the sofa, frowned

with suspicion. 'What sort of pictures?' she asked.

'They were taken by my great-uncle,' replied Grandma Kate. 'When he was in Africa.'

'Did they have cameras then?' asked Susy. I knew what she was thinking. Grandma Kate is pretty old, so this great-uncle must have lived hundreds of years ago.

'Well, they'd done the wheel, so I suppose the camera would have been next.' She laughed at her own wit. 'But cameras were more complicated then. Uncle Philip needed several bearers to carry his photographic equipment alone.'

Now this really did sound interesting. This was not a man who snapped a few moth-eaten lions from the safety of a safari truck. Anyone who had bearers was into serious pioneering.

Grandma Kate stood on a chair and took the album down from the top of the book-case. She dusted it with a tissue and sat down between Susy and me on the sofa.

'These,' she said, reverently tapping the leather cover. 'These pictures were in the *National Geographic* all those years ago.'

'What's the national geographic?' asked Susy.

'It's an important magazine,' I said with

supreme knowledge. My mum told me about it one day when we picked up an old copy in the dentist's waiting-room. You know how it is, you'll read any old thing in the dentist's waiting-room. And I mean old. Dad says if you spend long enough in a dentist's waiting-room you end up in a time warp and find yourself saying things like, 'Those Beatles are fab!' or 'Shame about the Titanic.'

'This national magazine,' Susy nudged me. 'What is it?'

'*National Geographic*. It's all about the world and...and animals and things.'

Susy gave me a look. 'Yeah,' she scoffed. 'Brill. You can get all that on the Net.'

Grandma Kate was turning the pages. Each page was separated by very fine tissue. Susy peered closer. 'They're all dull and brown!' she exclaimed.

And so they were. But I wasn't about to let Susy knock everything. 'They were taken at a time when photography was primitive,' I said. 'Try and let your feeble mind grasp the fact that modern technology had to begin some-where.' Sometimes my own eloquence surprises even me.

'Right,' agreed Grandma Kate. 'Prints came out brown all those years ago. These,' she tapped the album again, 'are valuable records of parts of Africa where no white man had been before.'

'Wow!' Now I was seriously impressed. 'I wish I could have lived then and gone with him,' I said.

Susy snorted. 'Then he wouldn't be your great, great, great, great great-uncle,' she said. 'And anyway you'd be dead by now, though that would be just fine as far as I'm concerned.'

'Do you want to see these or not?' said Grandma Kate impatiently. 'I have other things I can be doing if you two just want to snipe at one another.' She closed the album.

'Yes!' we both chorused.

'I'm really interested,' I added. 'Really, Grandma Kate.'

'All right then,' she said, opening the album again, turning the pages carefully. There were photos of the African landscape, lions, giraffes, monkeys and crocodiles. But the really interesting ones were the photos of natives standing outside their primitive huts.

'Why are those people hiding their faces?' asked Susy. Sure enough, all of the natives in the pictures were holding their hands or shields or bits of cloth up to their faces. It was pretty strange.

'Is it that they were so ugly that Great-uncle Philip was afraid they'd break the camera?' I joked.

Grandma Kate shook her head, didn't laugh at my joke. 'They'd never seen a white man before, let alone all the paraphernalia that went with taking photographs. Can't you imagine their consternation at seeing all this "magic" being set up?'

'But why hide their faces?' asked Susy.

'Because they thought that Great-uncle Philip was capturing their spirits in his camera,' explained Grandma Kate. 'His big mistake was that, before taking their photos, he tried to explain what he was doing so he showed them some pictures he'd taken of other people. That sent them into a tizzy. They thought that the people were trapped inside those photos and that the same thing would happen to them if they showed their faces.'

'Just think of how they'd react to a telly,' laughed Susy. 'They'd have been thoroughly spooked.'

'And so would Great-uncle Philip,' I said.

'True,' agreed Grandma Kate. 'Like I'm spooked by all this Internet stuff and cyberspace. It's all a question of the time you happen to be born in relation to technological progress.'

I looked at Susy to see if she knew what Grandma Kate was on about and was relieved to see that she hadn't understood either. I hoped she wouldn't ask for an explanation because I wanted to get back to the natives with no faces. I peered even closer, but there wasn't one face to be seen.

'Do you know,' continued Grandma Kate, 'in one village Great-uncle Philip only got away with his life by throwing the plate from the camera into the fire. The people were happy when they saw the smoke. They thought it was their spirits released from "the spirit box" – as they called the camera.'

'Why didn't he tell them that he was only taking their picture?' asked Susy. 'Surely they'd have understood if he really explained.'

Grandma Kate shrugged. 'Those were dangerous times for explorers,' she said. 'Remember most of these people hadn't seen a white man before. They had their own culture, their own way of life. Naturally they were suspicious of these strange men with their funny gadgets. All the explanations in the world wouldn't shake them from their own superstitions. You can't blame them for thinking that their spirits would be sucked into a weird thing like a camera.'

For some reason the pictures of these frightened people hiding their faces was making me uneasy. I gave another one of those shivers that seemed to be firmly stuck in the back of my neck by now.

'Why, Arty, you're cold,' said Grandma Kate. 'I think the night has changed.' She got up to close the windows.

Outside it had got very dark, even though it was only nine-thirty. The wind had whipped up, making the curtains flap noisily. 'Listen to that,' went on Grandma Kate, struggling against the swirling curtains. 'The weather forecast was for warm sunny weather – it *is* supposed to be summer after all. Can't trust those weather gismos up in the sky, can you? Turn on the telly now, Susy, and let's see if there's any mention of storms.'

But when the weather report came at the end of the news, there was no mention of storms. By now the wind was really moaning and the rain tap-tapped on the window.

'See what I mean?' laughed Grandma Kate. 'Weather forecast how are ye!'

'Could we watch the film on the other channel?' asked Susy, adding, 'The *only* other channel,' just to drive home the fact that entertainment was thin on the ground.

'Go ahead,' said Grandma Kate, putting the album back on top of the bookcase. 'I like Superman. Anyone like some ice-cream? I'll get some from the freezer. You two punch up the cushions and we'll pig out and watch the movie.'

My nerves were beginning to feel so freaky

that I jumped when the sitting-room door squeaked loudly as Grandma Kate came back with the ice-cream.

She noticed my nervousness. 'Must oil that silly door,' she said.

I tried to focus on the film. It was the first of the Superman movies and I hadn't seen it since I was eight. But that uneasy feeling wouldn't go away. And the moaning wind was beginning to do my head in. Maybe, I tried to console myself, maybe it will simply blow itself out. But it didn't. In fact it seemed to howl even more loudly and the rain tapped more frantically.

Half way through the film, the electricity blacked out.

6

We sat in stunned silence for a moment, not quite believing what had happened.

'Just what we need!' muttered Grandma Kate. 'Now, where did I put the candles? This is what happens; you put things in a safe place and then, when you need them, you can't remember where that safe place was.'

I could feel the sofa springs move as she got up, and I jumped up too. There was no way I was going to sit here with just Susy for protection. Not with that racket going on outside and a blanket of scary dark inside.

'Hold on, Grandma Kate,' I cried. 'I'll help you look for them.'

'Me too,' said Susy. I could feel her reach out and clutch one side of Grandma Kate's cardigan. I was clutching the other side. This was no time for solitary heroics. The three of us shuffled along the hall to the kitchen, Susy and Grandma Kate giggling like a couple of loonies. The kitchen was completely dark. Except for the lingering smell of the chips we'd had for tea, we wouldn't have known we were in the kitchen. Strange how the most familiar place loses its friendly vibes when conditions change it. We felt our way along the kitchen unit, knocking over things like the mug tree and the cutlery carousel which clattered into the sink.

'Good job I didn't leave the Waterford glasses here,' said Grandma Kate.

'Grandma Kate, you don't have Waterford glasses,' said Susy. 'You gave them to my mum because you said you preferred chunky pottery, remember?'

'Well, isn't that lucky then? At least we know they're safe.'

Susy laughed, her disembodied voice tinkling in the dark. 'You're cracked, Gran,' she said. 'You say the weirdest things.'

'Look, couldn't we just get the candles?' I put in. I was not enjoying this silly conversation. *Someone* had to be logical and sensible and I was the only candidate.

Grandma Kate stooped to pull out a drawer in the unit and I lost my grip on her cardigan. As I reached out to grasp it again, a blue flash of lightning lit up the kitchen. It was only for a nano second, but it was long enough for me to glimpse shadowy movements in the garden. Shapes that flickered across the grass. Lumpy, formless shapes. Several glaciers descended on the back of my neck.

'Look!' I croaked. 'Did you see them?'

'Yes, I have them here,' said Grandma Kate as she eased herself upright. 'I knew they had to be ...'

'No! Those figures outside! Did you see those figures moving outside?'

'Get lost, Arty,' growled Susy. 'There's no need to try and scare...'

'But I *did* see something moving. I did! I'm not a complete eejit...'

'Ha!' scoffed Susy.

Grandma Kate struck a match and lit one of the candles. She held it up and leaned forward to pull back the net curtain on the window. All we could see was the reflection of the three of us. She lowered the candle.

'Nothing, lad,' she said. 'There's nothing out there. You must have imagined it. Lightning can play tricks on your eyes. Now, let's get some more of these candles lit and I'll phone the electricity people to tell them we've lost power.'

'I didn't imagine it,' I persisted. 'I did, Grandma Kate... I did see things moving out there.'

'Oh, shut up,' put in Susy. 'Joke's over.'

Grandma Kate put her hand on my head. 'It's just the trees, pet,' she said soothingly. 'Listen to that wind, it would make anything move.'

She nearly convinced me. Only nearly.

'Let's lock all the windows and doors,' I said. 'Just...just in case.'

'Oh, for crying out loud!' Susy exploded. 'I'll strangle you, Arty Adams. I swear I'll strangle you. You don't know when to stop, do you?'

'Sshh,' said Grandma Kate, handing us a candle each. 'Arty's right. We'll lock up.'

I knew she was only doing it to humour me, but I didn't care. We went on another shuffling expedition, closing windows and locking the front and back doors.

'Look!' exclaimed Susy. 'Moving shapes! Oh help!'

I felt the blood drain from my face. Had those shapes somehow got in? Before I could pass out in a dead faint, Susy began to cackle and point to the distorted shadows we were casting in the candlelight.

'Ha, I knew it!' she gloated. 'You're afraid of shadows, you dork.' She made one hand into a clawlike shape and held the candle behind it so that its shadow looked like a giant talon on the wall.

'Oooohhh,' she moaned. 'Helllppp...'

'Give over, Susy,' said Grandma Kate. 'Like you said, joke's over. Better check on my studio in case that rain gets in. Come on.'

The candlelight quivered as we made our

way back down to the kitchen and into Grandma Kate's studio. The fury of the storm seemed much louder here. Probably because of all the glass, I told myself. The glass doors were rattling loudly and there was a dripping sound coming from one corner.

'Well, would you look at that,' said Grandma Kate, holding her candle aloft. My first response was to bury my head in my sweater, but I forced myself to look. 'Blasted wind has broken a pane of glass,' she went on. Sure enough, there was a jagged hole in one of the upper panes through which the rain was steadily dripping.

'Must have been a branch of a tree that blew against it,' said Susy. 'Or maybe a dragon,' she added, looking at me, making that talon shape with her hand again.

'I must get the picture I'm working on to a safer place,' said Grandma Kate. 'Here, Arty, you hold my candle while I move the picture in case more glass breaks. The rain would destroy it.'

She took the hedgehog picture off the easel and put it under her arm. Then she reached out for the large sketchbook in which she had been drawing the tree earlier – it seemed like a hundred years ago. Just then there was another flash of lightning.

I glanced through the window. With my

heart bouncing off my stomach I recognised the same darting, flickering shapes. I tried to tell myself that Grandma Kate was right, that it was the trees moving. But these were not trees. I knew that well enough by now.

'There!' I cried triumphantly. 'You must have seen them that time. Moving shapes.'

Susy said something rude. Grandma Kate peered into the dark outside and shook her head in the candlelight. 'No, son. Like I said, it's just the wind in the trees. Don't let this silly old storm get to you. It will be over soon. Come on, let's get to the phone and get those electricity people to put us out of our misery.'

I was relieved when we got to the phone. Now somebody would come and fix the electricity. I hoped they'd send a whole gang of repairmen. I'd tell them about the shapes and they'd look around with their big torches. Repairmen always carry powerful torches. Thanks to the prospect of contact with the real world, I was beginning to feel normal again – a normality which made me think that maybe those shapes were nothing more than tricks of the light after all. I held the candle below my chin and stuck out my top teeth to make a vampire face.

'Gotcha!' I nudged Susy. She gave me a scathing look and mouthed the word 'prat'.

Grandma Kate dialled and listened. Then

she dialled again and looked anxious. She pressed the button thing that the receiver rests on and dialled again. My heart started on its journey down to my stomach again. I swallowed hard, afraid to ask the question I knew she was going to answer anyway.

'Not a peep,' she said. 'No sound. Dead as a dodo. Lines must be down.'

'Oh shoot!' said Susy. 'Now we won't even see the rest of Superman.'

Superman! I could have done with a visit from that man, red Y-fronts and all.

'Try again, Gran,' I said, trying very hard to keep the panic out of my voice. 'Just once more. Are you sure it's plugged in right?'

She handed me the receiver. 'You try.'

I shut my eyes and willed the dial tone to give a comforting hum. No such luck. I pressed the buttons frantically – any buttons, just to get a reaction.

'No point in doing that, love,' said Grandma Kate, taking the receiver from me and putting it back on its cradle. 'Never mind,' she went on, trying to inject a bright note into the situation and failing miserably. 'They'll fix everything tomorrow. They could even fix it tonight. We could find the lights suddenly coming on. That often happens when the electricity goes.'

Her voice tapered off when she saw the two

scared faces looking miserably up at her. At least it was a very slight consolation to see that Susy was scared too.

'I hate this,' she muttered. 'I hate all this dark and the howling wind and rain. What'll we do, Grandma Kate?' She looked almost accusingly at Grandma Kate in the flickering candlelight, as if it was all the old lady's fault.

Grandma Kate shrugged. 'Not a lot we can do,' she said. 'Sit it out, I expect. Tomorrow will be grand. What about a picnic tomorrow?'

Susy glowered again. 'We have to get through tonight first,' she said. 'You can't have a tomorrow without a tonight and I'm not very happy with this tonight.'

Grandma Kate sighed and looked at the hall clock with exaggerated deliberation. 'After ten,' she said. 'It's bedtime already. Why don't we just go to bed and sleep our way through this. You two must be tired.'

The thought of being banished to my own bedroom, alone in the middle of this scarifying scenario was not a delightful prospect. Happily it was Susy, outspoken Susy, who knocked that idea on the head.

'Are you daft, Gran?' she exclaimed. 'If you think for one crazy minute that I'm going to split from the rest of the party you can think again. This cruddy storm is freaking me out.'

'Okay,' said Grandma Kate. 'You can come

into my bed, how about that?'

I swallowed hard. Great. Those two could snuggle up together while I got murdered in my dark, lonely room. My hair would probably turn white with fear and horror. Before I got murdered, that is.

Surprisingly enough it was Susy who saved my bacon – and saved me the embarrassment of pleading for mercy.

'And Arty,' she said. 'Arty must come too.'

I was touched by her consideration. That is until she looked at me and added, 'Anyway, he's a boy. If there's any weird stuff going on we can send him to investigate. That's what boys are for.'

Charming. I was merely spook bait.

Grandma Kate laughed. 'There will be no weird stuff, as you call it, Susy. It's only a summer storm. Come on, you can both sleep in my bed. We can pretend that it's a covered wagon out in the Wild West in the middle of a storm. Now take your candles, the two of you, and go wash your teeth. I'll go as far as the bathroom with you and then I'll just put these pictures in a safe place.'

7

Although it was pretty reassuring to be snuggled up with Grandma Kate and Susy under the big downy duvet, I still didn't sleep very well. What made it worse was that the other two seemed to have been lulled by the moaning wind into snoring slumber.

That's one of the really grotty things about being with other people and not being able to sleep. Like the first time you go camping with the cub scouts and everyone else in the tent is snoring their silly heads off while you spend the night tossing and fretting. It's like the whole world is closing in on you. Well, that was how I felt now. Only this was worse – the whole world *was* closing in on me. And there was the added worry that Susy would tell my mates that I'd been too scared to sleep on my own during a stupid old storm.

I wished Grandma Kate would wake up and tell me again that everything would be all right. I even stuck my bony elbow under her chin, but she just muttered and turned away. I tried to shut out the sounds of the storm by burying my head under my pillow. Then I tried taking really deep breaths. That seemed to work, I fell into a nice, relaxing doze and floated from there into real sleep.

It was coming on to the bluey light of early dawn when I was jolted awake. The storm had died down a little bit. But what had wakened me? I peeked over the duvet and saw the flimsy curtain blowing in a ghostly form at the window. I smiled to myself with relief, nothing to worry about in that.

I was snuggling down to try and catch the rest of my sleep before it got away when I heard a faint tinkling sound coming from downstairs. I froze. Please let me have imagined it. But there! There it was again – the distinct sound of breaking glass. I nudged Grandma Kate.

'Wake up, Grandma Kate,' I said in a hoarse whisper.

'What is it?' she asked sleepily.

'There's someone downstairs trying to get in.'

'Hmmm?'

'Please, don't go to sleep again. Listen. There's someone trying to break in.'

Grandma Kate turned away from me and plumped her pillow before settling down again. 'You're imagining things again, lad,' she half yawned. 'Go back to sleep.'

This time there was no doubt. There was

another, louder tinkling of breaking glass. And this time Grandma Kate heard it too. I could feel her body become rigid. Suddenly she sat up. By now Susy was awake too.

'What's going on?' she groaned, wiping her eyes in the gloom.

'Sshh,' whispered Grandma Kate.

As if in echo to that, there was the unmistakable sound of hissing which could be heard over the dying wind.

Ssss...ssss... it went. A familiar sound. I knew I'd heard it before. The three of us jumped as more glass broke downstairs.

'What's that?' asked Susy.

Grandma Kate hopped out of the bed. I wished she hadn't. There was a great empty space where she'd been and this was not a time for empty spaces. We needed to huddle together. She turned towards Susy and me. Even in the blue-grey gloom I could see that her face was white and tense. She leaned forward and tucked the duvet around us.

'Listen to me,' she whispered. 'I don't know who's down there, but I'm damned if I'll let any young hooligan break into my house. I'm going down there to investigate.'

'No!' I cried. 'Don't go down there. Please don't go down there, Grandma Kate. Let them have what they want and go away.'

'He's right,' agreed Susy. 'I've seen on TV

about thugs who break into old people's houses and rob them. They beat them up and sometimes kill them. They're scumbags, Grandma Kate. Don't go down.'

Grandma Kate had put on a skirt and jumper and was now lacing up the shabby trainers that she wore in the bog. She gave Susy a wry smile. 'I'm not that old, sunshine,' she said. 'There's plenty of fight left in this old bird.'

Then she padded over to the wardrobe and took out a metal-tipped hurley. She waved it at Susy and me. 'Whoever is down there will rue the day they came up against a former all-Ireland camogie champ,' she said.

'Wait,' said Susy, jumping out of bed. 'I'm coming too. We'll smash their...'

'You'll do no such thing,' snapped Grandma Kate. She came over to the bed and peered at the two of us with great intensity. 'I want both of you to promise me that you'll stay here. Got that?'

'But...' began Susy.

'No buts,' insisted Grandma Kate, holding back the duvet for Susy to get back in beside me. 'You have to promise me, both of you, that you'll leave this to me. I'm a fine strong lump of a woman and I can fend for myself. Promise!'

Susy and I looked at one another and

reluctantly promised. I was confused. On the one hand I wanted to be at my gran's side, tackling whatever menace was downstairs. On the other hand I wanted to stay here, bury my head in the duvet and just hope that all this bad stuff would just go away.

Grandma Kate tiptoed across the room. At the door she stopped and looked back at us.

'Not to stir now,' she whispered. Then she softly opened the door and slipped out.

8

Susy and I sat in shocked silence after she'd gone.

'Arty, I hate this,' said Susy. 'I just hate it. She'll never manage to thump those nerds on her own. Why wouldn't she let us come? Together we'd make mincemeat of them.'

'We'd get in the way,' I replied. 'We're small, we'd get in the way. We'd cramp her style. She'll take a swing at them and send them flying.'

Susy looked at me. I knew I had botched that bit of supposedly solid common sense.

'You don't really believe that, do you?' she said. 'I can always tell when you're fobbing me off with a stupid answer … Arty Adams,' she went on, 'what are you really thinking?'

I swallowed and stared straight ahead, trying to concentrate on the flapping curtain.

'I don't think…' I began.

'You don't think what? Speak up.'

I cleared my throat. 'I don't think that they're thieves that are breaking in,' I went on, the words coming out in a rush.

'What? What are you talking about?'

I turned to look at Susy's scared face. She gave me a dig in the ribs with her fist. 'What are you saying? This is no time to be weird, for crying out loud.'

I shook my head. 'I wish – I hope, that it *is* only robbers. Human robbers.'

Susy took a sharp breath. 'What do you mean?' she whispered.

'All those shapes, Susy. You remember those shapes I said I'd seen?' She nodded her head, her eyes wide and frightened. 'Well, I didn't imagine them. They *were* out there.'

'And...and now you think they're in here?' Susy said hoarsely.

I nodded miserably. She suddenly hopped up and confronted me, her angry face inches from me. 'And do you mean to say that you've let Grandma Kate off on her own to face these...these demon things that you saw? You're actually sitting there, safe in bed, telling me that you're not worried about letting that dear old lady be spooked – murdered maybe – by these creatures? You're a mouse, Arty. God, if I'd known I'd have made sure to go with her.'

'You heard what she said,' I said, feebly trying to defend my actions, or rather, lack of actions. 'She made us promise...'

Susy was now out of the bed. 'Yeah, sure,'

she said. 'But that was before you said any-thing about spooks.'

'But I *told* you about them,' I said, still defensive. 'I told you both earlier. Not my fault if you wouldn't believe me.'

'You should have said. Before Grandma Kate left, you should have said.'

I sighed. This was a no-win situation.

'Well, you still wouldn't have believed me,' I muttered. 'What are you doing?'

Susy was pulling on her jeans. 'What do you think I'm doing, cowardy custard?' she said. 'I'm going down there after Grandma Kate. Spooks or robbers, I'm not going to let her take them on by herself. You coming or are you just going to sit there like a wimp?'

'I'm not a wimp,' I said, pushing back the duvet and grabbing my own clothes. We both froze when a hissing sound seemed to come from the hall. Susy looked at me. You could see that all her bravado had gone on hold. She gave a short whimper. Now was my chance to be one-up.

'If you're too scared I'll go by myself,' I said, hoping that the machine-gun that was my heart couldn't be heard as it ricocheted off my rib-cage. That shook Susy back to her tough self. 'Huh,' she said. 'As if!'

We both took a deep breath and quietly opened the door. The smell was the first thing that hit us. It was as though a million rotten things had been thrown into the hall below. It was the stink of decay and mustiness, of rotten vegetation and dead creatures. We gagged at the awfulness of it. Susy pressed her hand over her mouth. I put the neck of my sweatshirt over my mouth and nose, but still the smell got through.

I knew then, with absolute certainty, that whatever was downstairs, it was something seriously terrifying. Grandma Kate was in the worst possible danger. Susy was right, I groaned to myself. I should never have agreed to let her off alone. Well, by jingo I'd make up for it now. I grabbed Susy's arm.

'Quickly!' I cried. 'We've got to find Gran.'

Susy was infected by my sudden burst of courage. She took my hand and the two of us ran down the stairs. We drew up short when we saw, in the dawn light from the open front door, a splatter of total devastation in the hall. It was as if someone had dumped a whole skip of rubbish there. Apart from slimy tracks that led from the door along the whole length of the hall, there were bits of twigs and rotten leaves scattered about. The stench was at its worst here and we gagged again. The wind had completely died down and the hissing sound was gone. Susy snatched her hand from mine and ran to the door, stepping over the debris and shouting as she went.

'Gran! Gran, where are you?'

We both ran out into the garden. I nearly popped my clogs when I saw Grandma Kate's hurley lying on the wet grass, a root or branch twisted around it.

'Oh lord!' exclaimed Susy. 'Tell me this isn't happening.'

But it was. No amount of pinching would wake us up from this nightmare. I could see that there was only one thing to do.

'We've got to follow these tracks,' I said to Susy. 'Whoever – whatever – has Grandma Kate has left these tracks.'

Susy gave another whimper. 'Maybe they've gone and left her d...unconscious in the house. Let's check the house first.'

I knew we were wasting our time. I knew Grandma Kate had been taken away. But I followed Susy back into the devastated hall. We went from room to room. Surprisingly enough, the only messed up areas were the hall and Grandma Kate's studio. The studio was the worst. Easels had been turned over, paint tubes scattered on the slimy floor, jam jars lay broken and there were drawings and paintings lying in a soggy mess. But no Grandma Kate.

'I told you, Susy,' I said. 'Come on, we're wasting time here. We've got to follow those tracks. If we hurry...' I gulped at the thought that occurred to me. 'If we hurry we might catch them.'

'And if we do?' asked Susy, voicing the very fear that had made me gulp.

I shrugged. 'Dunno, but we have to go after them.'

'Yeah,' she agreed. 'That's all we can do. Come on. I'm dead scared, but what must it be like for her? She's alone out there with those...things.'

We went back outside and looked at the trail of slime and vegetation. It led into the forest, along the track that led to the bog. The bog with the spooky tree and ...

'I remember!' I exclaimed.

'Remember what?'

'That hissing sound we heard earlier. It's the same sound we heard that time when we saw those bubbles in the bog.'

Susy looked at me with disbelief. 'You mean...you mean that whatever was making those hissing sounds was here?'

I bit my lip and nodded.

'Oh lord, Arty. What are we up against?'

'We'll find out,' I said, looking along the trail we had to follow. 'Too darn soon, we'll find out.'

9

The track through the forest was gloomy. The rising sun hadn't managed to break through the thick foliage. Even if it had, I felt that it could not dispel the awful chill that was everywhere. The smell of rotten things was as strong as ever. It was more than a damp smell of decay, it seemed to seep right through our clothes and skin to our bones. It was almost as if we were part of the whole rotten scene.

'It's leading right back to the bog where we were yesterday,' said Susy.

'I know that,' I replied. But for once there was no triumph in already knowing something that Susy had just discovered.

As we drew nearer to the bog clearing we found ourselves in a thick mist. It was icy cold and we moved closer to one another both for warmth and reassurance. Susy clutched my hand.

'We'll be all right,' I said to her. I felt I had to be the strong one. 'We'll work this out. Don't be scared.'

'You're lying through your teeth, Arty,' she

said. 'And don't try to con me. You're more scared than I am. And don't treat me like I'm some wimpy kid. You know darn well that I'm tougher than you. I'm only holding your hand to protect you.'

'Yeah, well,' I replied. 'No harm in trying to put on a brave front, is there? Anyway, this is not a time to be fighting over who's braver than who. This is not a game.'

'Too bloomin' right,' said Susy. 'Truce then. We're both scared mindless, but we've got to see this through.'

Through the grey mist, the bog opened out before us. The mist seemed to be rising and wafting from the centre of the marshy area. Looking over at the gnarled old tree we could just make out its silhouette as it stood against the grey nothingness of the mist. There was enough of it visible to see that the roots were now even more bare. More than ever they looked like grasping fingers. That fridge door was positively opening and shutting with monotonously frightening regularity.

'It's to do with that tree,' I said to Susy.

'What is?'

'Whatever is going on, it's to do with that tree. That cruddy tree has been giving me the creeps since I first saw it.'

'Where's Grandma Kate?' said Susy, a sudden panic creeping into her voice. 'This trail of rotten stuff – look, it ends here right at the edge of the marshy bog. Do you think...?' She paused and looked at me with terror. 'Do you think she's been sucked under. Like my drawing. You remember the way my drawing was sucked under?'

I remembered. 'I don't know,' I admitted. 'But let's search around.'

We kept together and walked around the perimeter of the bog, calling and calling for Grandma Kate. Nothing. Not a sound. Not even the rustling of the trees. At one point, peering through the mist I saw Mr Kitt's Land Rover. My heart lifted. Was he here? He'd help us. But then I realised that it was in exactly the same position as it had been yesterday. That Land Rover had not moved from there. Here was fresh fear. Fridge door.

'Isn't that whatisface's truck?' asked Susy.

'Yes,' I said slowly. 'But I don't think he's around.' I didn't elaborate. No point in scaring the child.

'You mean he's been abducted by these spooks too,' she said. Sometimes she's too smart for her own good. Or mine.

By now we'd searched the whole grove around Grandma Kate's haven. If she was here, she'd have responded by now. With sinking hearts we realised that we'd done as much as was humanly possible. And I stress the word 'humanly'. By now we knew we weren't dealing with anything remotely human.

'Listen, Susy,' I said eventually. 'We've got to get help on this. There's nothing more a couple of kids like us can do. We've got to get to the village and tell someone. This is beyond us.'

I thought she'd throw a virago tantrum and insist on trawling the bog ourselves, but for once she showed a bit of sense.

'You're right,' she said. 'We'll have to get to some adults and tell them what has happened. Come on, we haven't time to lose.'

I breathed a sigh of some relief. At least I wouldn't have to argue with her.

'Let's go,' I said. 'We'll get to the village. It's about two miles, but we might get a lift. The sooner we put this in the hands of the gardai the better.'

We made our way back through the gloomy forest. That chill was still everywhere, but there was a small bit of consolation in the fact that we'd soon have help.

10

No cars passed us on our way to the village so we were pretty exhausted by the time we got there. There was something very reassuring about seeing ordinary people going about their ordinary affairs, shopping and chatting and swearing at bad driving.

The garda station was quiet. The desk sergeant looked up from his crossword when we came in. I knew he was doing a crossword because he had a dictionary like my dad has when he does the *Irish Times* crossword. He leaned forward when we came in.

'Well, come to give yourselves up, have you?' he said.

'Our granny's missing,' said Susy.

I hoped she wouldn't spew out her feminist venom at him. Susy likes to put people firmly in their place if they get up her nose.

'Ah,' said the garda. 'A missing granny, is it? Are you sure she's not giving you the slip? Maybe she's having a quiet little drink...'

Susy stood on her toes so that her nose was above the level of the high desk. 'Listen, mister,' she said. 'We're not being funny. Our gran has disappeared. We think that something from the bog has nabbed her. We're scared mindless, me and Arty.'

The garda folded his newspaper and leaned forward. 'Something from the bog, eh? A big old bogman, would you say?'

This was getting us nowhere. Time for me to put in a bit of sense. 'My cousin's right,' I said. 'Something slimy came out of the bog and took our gran away. After the storm last night...'

'Hold on there now, son,' said the garda, switching his attention to me. 'What storm is this? The weather has been balmy for the past week. We could do with a drop of rain.'

I looked at him in amazement. 'The storm last night,' I said patiently. 'There was thunder and lightning all night. You must have seen it.'

He was shaking his head. 'Afraid not. Which county were you in last night? We certainly hadn't a whisper of wind nor a drop of rain for weeks. I think maybe you two youngsters had better run along now. Tell your stories to someone who might believe you.'

He opened his crossword again, dismissing us. You don't do things like that with our Susy. She reached up and tapped the desk.

'Listen, mister,' she said. 'Me and my cousin have spent the morning looking for our gran. I'm telling you, something or someone has taken her away and we're scared out of our wits. If you don't do something about it I'll stand outside this cop shop and scream so much that a mob will gather.'

The garda sighed and put down his paper again.

'Okay, sweetheart,' he said. 'From the beginning. First of all, who is the granny that's missing?'

Susy dropped back to her normal height. 'She's Kate Adams,' she said, with a touch of pride. 'She's a famous artist.'

The garda rolled his eyes to heaven and smiled. 'I know who Kate Adams is,' he said. 'And I know that the same lady has been known to go missing at the drop of a hat. She goes off on a painting spree and forgets that there's a real world out here. Don't worry about her. She'll turn up. She should have told you she was going, but that's the sort of woman she is. Go on back to the cottage. She'll probably be there when you get back.'

'No,' I said. 'You don't understand, Guard. There was this storm. There were figures outside in the garden moving about. Then, early this morning, we heard glass breaking and Grandma Kate went to investigate. We 'haven't seen her since. You have to help us.'

'These figures,' the garda said, 'can you describe them. Tall? Short? What were they wearing?'

I clamped my mouth shut. Did he have to ask those questions?

Susy nudged me. 'Tell him, Arty.'

'No,' I whispered. 'I can't.'

Susy tut-tutted. 'I'll do it myself,' she hissed. She looked up at the garda. 'They weren't human,' she said. I cringed.

The garda's face brightened. 'Aha!' he laughed. 'Now we have phantoms in on the act. Attack of the Bogey Bogmen. You kids watch too much telly – the X-Files and all that mullarky. You should be out in the fresh air and you wouldn't be imagining all this rubbish.'

'It's true,' I muttered. 'Those figures were there. I saw them.'

'And you saw them too, little lady?' the garda said to Susy.

'No,' Susy replied. 'Just Arty. Me and Grandma Kate didn't see them. But if my cousin Arty says they were there, then they were there.'

The garda leaned as near to me as his big tummy would allow. 'See here, son,' he said with exaggerated patience. 'There was no storm, no ghosts. And your granny is known for her, er, bohemian ways. I'm telling you to go home and wait. She's probably off painting badgers or something. Off you go now, the pair of you.'

Susy kicked the bottom of the high desk. 'You think we're having you on,' she said in exasperation. 'Well, we're not. What do you take us for? We're deadly serious. Are you going to help us? Where's the head guard? I'm not leaving here until...'

At this stage the garda's expression changed from benign tolerance to impatient annoyance. This conversation was getting us nowhere. I caught Susy's arm before she had a chance to put her foot through the wood panelling and land us both in the slammer for vandalism.

'Come on,' I whispered. 'This is useless.'

The garda nodded approvingly. 'Now there's a sensible lad,' he smiled.

Susy glared, first at the garda, then at me.

'Wimp,' she hissed.

The garda bristled. 'Scoot,' he said. 'The pair of you.'

At that, I hauled the spitting cat that was my cousin out into the street.

11

'Listen,' I said, clamping my hand over Susy's mouth to try and smother any further insults. 'There's no point in trying to convince that creep. He doesn't believe us. Who could blame him, when you think about it? An old bird like Gran – known for her loony ways – goes missing and you and me, her blood relatives, come spouting about spooks and a phantom storm. What could he think except that we're a dotty family?'

Susy pushed my hand away, but at least she'd calmed down. 'I suppose so,' she muttered. 'So, what do we do now?'

I shuffled my feet, noticing the peat stains on my cheap trainers. 'Dunno,' I admitted. 'Go back, I suppose.'

Susy suddenly brightened. 'I know,' she said. 'We'll go to Kitt's place.'

'What? What's the point in doing that?'

'But don't you see?' she said crushingly. 'If he's there he might be able to help us. He might have seen something. If he did, then he could come back to the garda barracks with us and tell that nerd in there that there *is* weird stuff going on in the bog.'

'And if he's not there?'

Now it was her turn to shuffle her feet. 'If he's not, then it means that ... that whatever took Gran has taken him too.'

Were we really standing here, on an ordinary street, talking calmly about events so chillingly beyond anything we had ever imagined?

I shrugged. 'I still can't see the point,' I said. 'Anyway I know he won't be there. I was the last one to see him, remember?'

Susy stuck out her chin. 'Well, have you a better idea, cleverclogs? I know it's only a slim chance, but slim chances are all we have left.'

I sighed. She was right, though I hated to admit it. 'All right,' I said. 'Let's do it – even if it's a waste of time,' I added, just to take the triumphant look off Susy's face.

Kitt's house was about half a mile from the town. A long, pot-holed avenue led to a jumble of untidy outhouses around a cobbled yard that was littered with grotty furniture and rusty farm equipment. Somewhere a dog barked and Susy moved closer to me. No, I can't tell a lie – I moved closer to Susy. Well, being the one who'd have to do all the rational thinking in this scenario, I figured it was important that I stay safe.

The back of the house was at the other end of the yard. As we made our way towards it I saw the flicker of a grey net curtain on one of the ground floor windows.

'There's somebody there!' I said to Susy.

She nodded. 'See?' she said. 'I knew it was the right thing to do, to come here. Now maybe we'll get some answers.'

The dog barked again when we knocked on the peeling back door. We waited, looking at one another, but saying nothing. Then I knocked again. This time there was the shuffling sound of old feet on tiles. With a creak the door opened a fraction. One eye peered out at us.

'Well?' said a nervous, hostile voice.

A spaniel with droopy eyes thrust its head through the narrow opening and growled.

'Good doggie,' said Susy, bending down to pat the creature's head, making the woman open the door a little wider. The smell of boiled cabbage and old damp wafted out to meet us.

'What do you want?' the woman muttered. 'I'm very busy.'

Busy? Doing what? Certainly not house-cleaning, judging by the messy hall which was now in our line of vision.

'We wondered if we could speak to Mr Kitt,' I said, with over-the-top politeness.

Her eyes narrowed. She pushed a wisp of greasy hair behind her ear. She wasn't that old, not in a saggy, wrinkly kind of way, but there was an old aura about her.

'What d'ye want him for?' she asked.

Susy and I looked at each other, frantically searching for an answer that would make sense.

'We just want to ask him something about the bog,' I stammered. 'The bog out beyond the forest.'

'Oh yeah? What about the bog?' She was suddenly defensive. 'What's the bog got to do with you two?'

Boy, this biddy certainly packed a neat line of friendly repartee.

'Our granny is lost in the bog. We thought Mr Kitt might be able to tell us where she could be,' put in Susy. 'She sometimes goes painting in odd places and we thought Mr Kitt might know of some of those places.'

I nodded approvingly at Susy. She'd got the message across without once mentioning spooks and slime.

'Our granny is Kate Adams,' Susy went on.

A look of recognition flashed across the grim face at the door. The thin mouth widened into a witchy sneer. Any second now,

I thought, she'd point a finger at us and change us into frogs. Maybe that smell wasn't boiled cabbage and old damp, maybe it was a boiled Mr Kitt. You see how recent events had almost totally freaked my mind? I could believe anything at this stage. I shook my head to make it think more clearly.

'Oh, that one,' the woman snorted. 'She's trouble, she is. Always on about her stupid wildlife – interfering in people's business.'

She frowned and peered at us. 'Is that what you're at? Has she sent you two to torment my brother now? Well, you can just turn around. Go back and tell your daft granny that we won't budge...'

'That's not why we've come here,' Susy interrupted. 'Our granny is missing, like I said. We've got to talk to Mr Kitt.'

'Well, he's not here,' the woman snapped.

'Have you any idea where he is? When he'll be back?' I asked, shoving my foot a little nearer to the door.

'Get in here, Nero,' she shouted at the dog which had emerged and was jumping around Susy.

She had avoided my question. 'When did you last see Mr Kitt?' I persisted.

She looked up at me as she bent to pull the dog by his collar. 'This morning, of course. At breakfast. Look, the pair of you be off...'

69

'Was he in the Land Rover?' I put in. 'Did he leave in the Land Rover?'

'Yes. Yes, of course he took the Land Rover. He always uses the Land Rover for business. Look, I don't know what you two are after, or what your granny has put you up to, but you've no business snooping around here.'

'You can't have seen the Land Rover this morning,' said Susy triumphantly. 'The Land Rover has been parked in the bog since yesterday.'

A look of anxiety crossed the woman's face. 'What?' she exclaimed, off her guard with surprise.

'You haven't seen him today, have you, lady?' I said. 'You haven't seen him since yesterday.'

She went on the defensive again. Shoving the dog inside the door she turned to us angrily. 'Be off,' she said evenly. 'Before I call the gardai and tell them that you're trespassing.'

'Please *do* ring them,' said Susy. 'Maybe they'll believe us about our granny if you'll tell them that your brother is missing too.'

'Susy's right, Ms Kitt,' I added, doing the polite bit again. 'They don't believe us. If you were to tell them that Mr Kitt is missing too...'

'I'll do no such thing,' she retorted. 'My brother will turn up. He's often away on business. I don't need gardai snooping around as well as you two troublemakers.'

Fighting words, but I could see that we'd given her something to think about.

'He could be in danger,' said Susy. 'Last night there were spooky...'

She broke off when I nudged her. Whatever chance we had of getting this old bird on our side, talk of spooks and weird stuff would cut no ice.

'Please,' I said. 'Just ring and tell them that your brother didn't come home last night.'

'I will not.'

Realisation dawned on me. And on Susy.

'Because they come around here a lot, don't they?' she said, pointing to the lines of sheds. That did it. I groaned to myself. Ms Kitt's face turned puce.

'Go!' she ordered.

I took Susy's arm. 'No point in hanging on here,' I muttered. 'There's no way she's going to help now.'

Susy shrugged away my hand. 'You might never see your brother again!' she shouted as the door slammed. 'Silly cow,' she went on. 'More worried about the gardai coming here than about her brother going missing. Why did she tell a lie, saying she saw him this morning in his Land Rover?'

I nodded wisely. 'I'll bet she's used to telling lies for her brother,' I said scornfully. 'He's probably a small-time hustler on the side.'

'Like that fellow Greengrass in *Heartbeat*,' added Susy. 'Only a nasty version.'

'Whoever he is,' I replied, not wanting her to know I watch *Heartbeat* with my ma on Sunday nights.

I glanced back at the house just before we turned into the avenue. The curtain twitched again, but not before I saw the white, anxious face of Ms Kitt.

'We've certainly got her worried anyway,' I said.

'Well, we've plenty to worry about ourselves,' said Susy.

With sinking heart, I knew she was right. All the fears and horrors of last night rushed to mind in an overwhelming cloud of dread. Above all, there was the terrifying worry over what had happened to Gran.

12

We sat at a table outside Byrne's Cafe to try to get our thoughts together. Was there nobody who could help us? For a fleeting moment I felt angry at Gran for being such a well-known weirdo. If she was a normal old woman who played Bingo and knitted hats for boiled eggs, the gardai would probably have organised a search-party by now. I gave a deep sigh. Susy looked at me.

'It's a mess, isn't it, Arty?' she said.

I nodded. My face felt tight. 'I just don't know what to do next,' I said.

Susy stuck out her chin, so I knew some big decision was coming. 'We're going back into that garda station,' she said. 'It's their duty to find and protect people, so they can bloomin' well get up off their backsides and help us.' She pushed back her chair and got up, her wild hair quivering.

'Hold on, Su,' I said, reaching out to her. 'They won't believe us. They think we're making it up. It's no use...'

'Well, have you any other ideas?'

I shook my head.

'Well, then. Come on. I'm not going back to that house without having someone with us. No way.'

I sighed again and followed her. Outside the garda station she turned briefly and gave me a thumbs-up. 'Watch me,' she said.

The same garda was at the desk. He gave an exaggerated groan when he saw us.

'Oh no,' he groaned. 'The return of the vampire slayers.'

'See? I told you,' I hissed to Susy. But she wasn't listening.

'Mr Kitt is missing too,' she said. 'You can ring his sister. He didn't come home yesterday either.'

At that the garda threw back his head and laughed. I wished all the metal fillings on show would go radioactive and give him hell.

'Kitt, is it? Well, we all know about Kitt. Maybe he and your gran have eloped...'

'Cut the stupid jokes, garda,' spat Susy. 'We're telling you that two people are missing in the bog and all you can do is sneer. You're just a big fat...'

'What she means is that they could have fallen down a bog-hole,' I interrupted. 'Bogs can be dangerous places.' I looked intently at Susy, willing her not to bring up the spooky business again.

The garda leaned patiently across the desk. 'Listen, you two, I've had it up to here with your cock-and-bull story. Your gran, like I've already said, has been known to go to all sorts of hidden places for her pictures. And as for Mr Kitt,' he paused and gave a snort.' Kitt is, well, Kitt. Enough said. Now, I suggest you go home and wait for your...'

What happened next was really terrifying. Every nerve in my body jumped when Susy suddenly began hammering at the desk, wailing at the top of her voice. Both the garda and I froze into shock as she howled and wept.

'My granny is missing and nobody will help us to find her,' she screeched. 'Oh will someone please help. I'm sssoo scared for my gran. Me and my cousin,' sob, sob, 'are dead scared. Oh, this is terrible. I'm going out into the street to see if someone, anyone, will help us.'

That got attention all right! With one swift move the garda was on our side of the desk, restraining Susy from heading into the street with her hysteria in full flow.

'Ssshhh. Calm down, girl,' he soothed, awkwardly patting her arm. By now a couple more gardai had emerged from the inner office to see what the commotion was. He looked at them with embarrassment. 'It's okay,' he said. 'Everything's under control.'

'Doesn't sound much like it,' said a younger garda, nodding towards Susy who now had waterworks cascading down her face. I was lost in admiration. Was this Oscar-nomination acting or what!

'It's our gran,' she sobbed, wiping her tears with the back of her sleeve. 'Our old gran is missing and this man thinks it's funn...'

'Yes, yes. All right,' put in the desk garda, offering Susy a hanky. 'I'll come out to the cottage with you. Just stop crying, there's a good girl.' He looked at the other gardai who were watching with interest. 'Get back inside,' he said. 'I'll handle this. Murphy, you finish what you're at and take over the desk. I'll take these youngsters home.'

They sniggered and left. The garda looked at Susy, just narrowly missing the wink she'd given me. 'Come on. I'll take you both home. You'll be all right. We'll find your granny. But,' he added, glancing towards the office to check that none of the others were listening, 'if it's a thing that you're trying to put one over on me, I'll lock the two of you up and flush the key down the loo. Come on, then.' He took his hanky back from Susy (but not before she'd blown her nose several times to get the best value out of it).

'Ring Ms Kitt,' I said again. 'Her brother *is* missing. Go on. I know you don't believe us, but you'll believe her.'

'Yeah, yeah, I believe you,' said the garda in a rush, as Susy opened her mouth to wail again. 'I really believe you.'

If the situation hadn't been so horrible I'd have enjoyed the ride in the cop car. I'd have preferred it if the blue light was flashing and the siren wailing, but I figured he'd throw us out if we pushed our luck.

The two-mile drive to the forest only took a few minutes compared to the trudge Susy and I had made earlier. The sun was shining brightly and the path leading to Grandma Kate's was yellow and dusty. There was absolutely no trace of the heavy rain of the night before. Both Susy and I stiffened when the cottage came into sight. No mist. The flowers were waving in a gentle breeze.

'Wait till you see the hall,' said Susy. 'Wait till you see the slime and rotten stuff.'

The garda nodded doubtfully. He was fed up already. We got out of the car and rushed up the path. The front door was still open.

'See!' said Susy triumphantly. 'The front door is open.'

'That's probably because you forgot to close it,' said the garda. 'Did you close it?'

I shook my head sheepishly. I could not tell a lie. Well, yes I could, but what was the point? The man thought we were a couple of airheads anyway.

'Well, then. Nothing strange about that. You shouldn't leave a house door open. No knowing what weirdos are about.'

'That's just what we've been telling you!' I cried.

'Yeah, yeah,' muttered the garda. 'Let's get on with it.'

Susy ran ahead into the hall. She stopped suddenly and gasped. As I did when I caught up with her. The hall was as clean as the proverbial whistle. Not a twig nor a slime in sight.

'Well now,' said the garda. 'Where's this rotten stuff you mentioned?'

We didn't reply, but went down to the studio. Same story. It was messy all right, but no more messy than when Grandma Kate was working there. Susy and I looked at one another with total puzzlement.

'It was here,' I began lamely. 'There was a complete mess of slime and bits of twigs.' I felt I was fighting a losing battle.

Then I saw the broken pane of glass. 'Look!' I shouted exultantly.

The garda looked up at the hole and shook his head. 'Too high up for a forced entry,' he said. 'No one would try to break in from that height. That's just where a branch hit it some time ago. See?' he indicated the floor. 'No broken splinters.'

My shoulders sank even further and I began to doubt my own sanity.

He made his way around the house, calling out, 'Mrs Adams, Mrs Adams.' He opened cupboards and looked under tables.

'The phone,' cried Susy. 'The phone and the electricity were knocked out in the storm.' I brightened a little. Maybe now he'd know there had been a storm.

He made a grim sort of smile. 'Yeah, the storm,' he said. 'That phantom storm.' He flicked the hall switch. Light. Then he picked up the phone. We could hear the dial tone as it passed through his ear. Finally he frowned at the two of us. I cowered. Susy stuck out her puny chest. 'Well, you've come this far so you might as well come to the bog with us.'

The garda looked at his watch. 'Right. I'm only doing this for the sake of your granny,' he said. 'I wouldn't have her say that I was anything but nice to her grandchildren. Come on.'

He strode ahead of us to the clearing. Still no mist. The birds were singing and there was the smell of woodbine. Nobody spoke. The garda was peed off with this whole exercise and we were scared and confused. We caught up with him as he stood at the edge of the clearing. The bog looked peaceful. The heather was bright purple and the shrubs were bright green. I almost expected Grandma Kate to be sitting sketching that tree. The tree! I glanced over at it, ready to draw the garda's attention to its eeriness. But it looked pretty normal. Okay, it was still a gnarled old tree with whorls and roots, but it was anything but eerie just now.

But I *did* see something that might give credibility to our story. At the other side of the bog was Mr Kitt's Land Rover, exactly as it had been parked yesterday.

'Look, there's Mr Kitt's truck,' I urged, tugging at the garda's sleeve. He looked over.

'So?' he said. 'What's unusual about that? He does own the bog, after all,' he added sarcastically. 'He's got every right to park in his own bog.'

'But you see,' I went on, 'he disappeared yesterday too. One minute he was walking to his truck, the next minute he disappeared.'

'Well, he certainly hasn't disappeared now,' said the garda. 'And his sister hasn't rung us to say he's missing. Looks like your spooks haven't grabbed him.' He raised his arm and waved.

'What do you mean?' I asked.

'It's Mr Kitt,' gasped Susy.

Sure enough, a figure was waving from inside the Land Rover. It *did* look like Mr

Kitt, but I couldn't be sure. 'Let's go over and talk to him,' I said. 'He might know where Grandma Kate is...' I broke off as the garda leaned over to me.

'Listen, young fella-me-lad,' he said. 'I've had it up to here with your stories of storms and spooks and slime and a missing granny. Get yourselves back to your cottage and wait for your granny there. I don't have time for fantasy. I've told you, she'll turn up. I've lost count of the number of times the postman or the milkman reported that lady as missing, only to have her turn up bright and breezy after a few hours. Your gran is a bit on the wild side. Don't take any notice. Make some sandwiches or go play in the woods or something. The law doesn't take kindly to people dreaming up fairy-tales, just you remember that. Now, come on. I don't want to see or hear from you two again, okay?'

I could see that Susy was about to launch into an attack, but I stopped her.

'It's no use,' I whispered. 'He just won't believe us. There's no point.'

'But he *has* to believe us,' she replied, desperation in her voice. She shrugged herself free and ran after the striding figure of the garda. 'Listen, Guard,' she said. 'You must stay with us. We're terrified, Arty and me. Please stay.'

The garda stopped and bent down to pat her head. 'Look, sweetheart, I'm really sorry your granny is irresponsible enough to take off and leave you two, but I can't do any more about it. She's not a missing person, she's just a bit on the dotty side and has gone off to do one of her pictures. The best you and the lad can do is make the most of your time. Play some games. The forest is a great place for games. Just don't go wandering off, or your gran will be the one coming in to me to report *you* missing. She'll be back later and everything will be all right.'

He stood up straight in a very garda-like authoritative pose. 'And you can tell her from me, Garda Grogan, that she's not to leave you on your own like that again, okay? Look,' he went on, softening to Susy's fresh tears, 'If she hasn't come back by nine o'clock this evening you ring me and we'll organise a manhunt – womanhunt even.' He gave a forced laugh at his own feeble joke. 'Does that put your mind at ease?'

Susy nodded. Then Garda Grogan turned and made his way along the track. Helplessly we watched him going and realised we were on our own again.

Then I remembered the figure that had been waving from the Land Rover.

'Mr Kitt!' I shouted. 'Let's get Mr Kitt!'

But when we got across to the Land Rover, there was nobody inside it. A branch was pressed against the window on the passenger side.

'How could we have been so stupid as to think that this was someone waving?' asked Susy impatiently.

'It really did look like a person,' I groaned. Maybe we were meant to think that. But I didn't say that to Susy. She'd either freak out or else thump me for suggesting it.

13

Susy sank down on the grass. 'I can't take any more of this,' she said. 'I think I'll just sit here and die.'

I certainly didn't want to hang around here. 'Come on,' I said. 'We'd better do as he says. There's nothing more we can do, short of dragging the bog.'

We both looked out at the marshy bog. As we did, a shadow fell over it, as if someone had thrown a big bucket of grey paint. Fridge-door!

'Let's go,' I said, not even glancing towards the tree in case there might be some new and weird development there. Susy didn't need any more prompting. She was up like a shot. We ran around the perimeter of the marshy bog and raced down the path we'd come up.

I half hoped Garda Grogan might have had a change of mind but no. When we got to the cottage we were just in time to see the cop car bump over the uneven path to the road.

'What do we do now?' asked Susy.

I sighed. 'Do as he says, I suppose,' I said. 'Maybe he's right. Maybe Grandma Kate will turn up like she always does. We'd better stay close to the cottage.'

'No,' said Susy. 'I'm on for going back to the village.'

I looked at her and shook my head. 'What's the point in that?'

'We could tell someone else,' she went on. 'Get someone to come back here and stay with us.'

'Don't be daft,' I snorted. Although the idea of a third party was attractive. Especially some brawny and brainy adult who'd sort out this spooky mess. 'What would we say to them? Tell them about the storm that wasn't and the slime that isn't and the figures that aren't? You saw that garda's reaction. Nobody would believe us. Anyway I don't know anyone in the village. Do you?'

She shrugged. 'The man in the shop.'

'Yeah, right, Susy. He's sure to leave his customers and come out to look for someone who's well known as a loopy old bird and who disappears at the droop of a rabbit's ear.'

'Stop calling Grandma Kate a loopy old bird,' snapped Susy.

I know I shouldn't have said it like that, but I was angry and frustrated. And very scared. Maybe I was blaming Grandma Kate for living here, for being a nutter, and for having got us stuck in this bad scene.

Susy suddenly brightened. 'The phone!' she cried. 'The phone's back. We can ring home!'

A great feeling of relief washed over me. 'Your folks,' I said. 'Mine are in Wales, which is why I'm here facing all these horrors. But your folks will do fine. They'll sort us out. Come on.'

We ran around to the back door because Garda Grogan had locked the front one. Susy grinned at me as she picked up the receiver and listened to the totally mega-beautiful sound of the dial tone. She dialled. I could hear the phone ringing. She gave me a thumbs-up sign. We waited. And waited. Susy hopped from one leg to the other.

'Come on,' she muttered. 'Answer, one of you.' She let it ring out until we heard the blips.

I swallowed hard. 'Try again,' I suggested. 'Maybe they're out in the garden and didn't make it back to the house in time.'

Susy took a breath and we went through the whole heart-sinking procedure again.

'They're not there,' she said flatly.

'What about their mobile?' I asked.

Susy gave me a scathing look. 'Mum won't have one. Says they scramble your brains.'

'Oh yeah?' I said. 'Well if she'd move with the times *we* wouldn't be in danger of getting scrambled. Us and Grandma Kate.'

Susy slammed down the phone. 'Well, Mister Smartass, if you know so much why don't you ring your folks in Wales, eh?'

My shoulders sagged. 'I don't know where they are,' I said lamely. 'They're touring.'

'Typical,' said Susy. 'What was supposed to happen in an emergency? Supposing you died or broke your silly neck or something, what would have happened then? Stupid to go away like that and not leave a number.'

'Grandma Kate has a contact number,' I muttered.

'But she's not here, is she?'

'Look, this is getting us nowhere,' I put in. 'We're stuck here. We'll just have to muddle through on our own. Or...'

'Or what?'

I took a deep breath. 'Or we could scarper.'

Susy's eyes widened. 'Do you mean run away?' she asked.

'That's usually what scarper means,' I said. 'We could hitch-hike home to your place and get away from all this.'

Susy bit her lip thoughtfully. 'I don't know,' she said after a few moments. 'You heard what that garda said. He told us to stay around the cottage. If we hitch-hike we could be kidnapped by some loony who'd cut our throats. Anyway, think of the almighty fuss when our folks would find out we'd put ourselves in that kind of danger.'

'And what about the danger we're in now?' I said, with more than a tad of sarcasm.

'Not really,' said Susy. 'Garda Grogan said to ring him if Grandma Kate hasn't come back by nine. The phone is working so we'll be looked after by him. I think we should stay, Arty. Can't you see how we'd make things far worse by scarpering?'

I knew that what she was saying made sense, but a big part of me wanted to get as far away as possible. Here we were, so confused that within minutes of Susy suggesting we go away and me opting for staying, now *she* wanted to stay and *I* was the one who wanted to go.

We stood in a kind of uneasy truce for a few seconds. Susy shook her flaming curls and headed for the kitchen. 'Let's get something to eat,' she said. 'We're going to need our strength to sit it out until nine o'clock.'

We made some ham sandwiches and cut up the rest of the chocolate cake. I wished we could go back to yesterday when the three of us were here munching that cake. When the three of us had a life.

'Do you think we might have imagined it?'

asked Susy through a mouthful of roughly cut ham. 'Do you think the whole thing was just a filament of our imagination?'

'Figment,' I corrected her automatically, like I always do.

She scowled. 'Whatever. Anyway, do you think we could have imagined it all, the slime and the storm and everything? You hear of people, loads of people, imagining weird things together. Like moving statues or UFOs.'

'And all their grannies disappearing?' I said sarcastically.

'No, think about it, Arty,' went on Susy. 'She could have got up early this morning to see some flowers or animals at dawn. She does that – we all know that's the sort of thing she does. Well, maybe last night was just a bad dream that you and I had. Maybe there was something in this...' she looked with distaste at the slice of chocolate cake she'd picked up and dropped it on her plate. 'That could be it ... *must* be it! Don't you see? Grandma Kate is so weird she could have mistakenly put something strange into the cake and we've simply been imagining everything. Probably used turps or acrylic paint instead of proper cooking stuff. Arty,' she leaned excitedly towards me, 'it makes sense, doesn't it? Look around you. There is absolutely nothing to show for what we thought happened. What do you say?' She reached out and shook my arm.

'I'm thinking, I'm thinking,' I said. I looked at the cake that Grandma Kate had told us she'd made specially for us. What Susy was saying certainly made a lot of sense. There *have* been many cases where gangs of people experienced, or thought they experienced, the same phenomena after eating weird mushrooms or doing drugs. I smelled the cake. It smelled of chocolate.

'You wouldn't smell it, silly,' said Susy. 'You probably wouldn't even taste it.'

I tried to reason out all the things she'd said and the more I thought, the more it made sense. Everything that had happened had felt so real and yet, when you'd think about it, so *unreal* that you felt it couldn't possibly have happened. And yet...

'The mist...' I began. 'And the tree. That spooky tree.'

'The mist was just condensation,' said Susy. 'Grandma Kate said so, don't you remember? And the spooky tree is only showing more roots because the dry weather has made the ground around it shrink. Grandma Kate said that too.' She was leaping around with excitement now.

'But that storm,' I went on. 'It was so real. And the figures I saw...'

'The figures *you* saw,' insisted Susy. 'Only you. And you ate more cake than any of us, like the greedy pig you are. And, as for the storm, it was probably only a shower, made worse by Grandma Kate's poisoned cake.'

'You could be right,' I said, beginning to share her excitement. 'Hell's bells, kid, you could be right.'

Susy laughed and emptied the rest of the cake into the bin under the sink. 'I am right. I know I'm right. There isn't even a smell. Do you remember the smell we *thought* we got this morning? How could a stink and a mess like that just disappear?' she said, snapping her fingers. 'It would have taken a hundred people days to clean up that mess and yet it all disappeared in a puff. Grandma Kate probably left the front door open and a few twigs and things blew in. See, Arty? She'll come back and we'll laugh over her funny chocolate cake. Am I glad I thought of this before we ate any. We don't want any more halleluias...'

'Hallucinations. No, we certainly do not.'

14

We watched telly for a bit, one of us nipping to the window every now and then to see if our granny might trip along the garden path with drawings of some silly bunnies or warty toads under her arm. I didn't know whether I'd hug her with relief or scream at her for putting Susy and me through this nightmare.

Half-past eight came.

'Another half hour,' I said. 'Another half hour and we ring Garda Grogan.'

Susy pulled her sweater down over her knees as she crouched on the sofa. With her red mop on top she looked like one of those round candles you'd have on the dinner-table at Christmas.

'Well, at least he'll come and get us looked after,' she said. 'We might be taken to a children's home. They do that with neglected kids, Arty. Or maybe he'll give us a cell in the cop shop. Wouldn't that be cool? We'd get to spend a night in the nick. Wow! I'd love that.'

'Give over,' I said. Still, it would be nice to be in a place where no spooks would venture.

If there *were* spooks. But I was having serious doubts in that quarter. Poisoned chocolate cake seemed like a reasonable cause of last night's hoo-ha. Good job I'm a very practical person. I know that some poisons can make people do funny stuff, so Grandma Kate's weird cooking could blow anyone's mind. Good job it didn't kill us.

We watched a silly quiz show and were unable to answer any of the questions. Then we sniggered at some old men playing diddly-eye music. Rivetting stuff, but right now I'd have settled for a dandruffy politician giving a party political broadcast to keep my mind from running amok.

Five minutes to nine. Five minutes for our gran to return or we were in the capable, adult, dependable hands of the men in blue.

At three minutes to nine we heard the first blustery moans of the wind.

At two minutes to nine the rain beat against the window.

Susy looked at me from her rolled-up position on the sofa.

'Ring him!' she cried. 'For crying out loud, Arty, ring Garda Grogan!'

I tried to swallow, but my jaws wouldn't work. Nothing worked. Fridge door.

Susy was off the sofa and into the hall before I could catch breath. Just before I ran out of the sitting-room door after her, the telly blanked out. And the light.

Susy was standing with the phone in her hand. She was furiously punching the buttons.

'That won't do!' I cried. 'All the numbers will run into one another. Take it easy, Su.'

She looked at me, terror written large all over her ten-year-old mush. She dialled again, exercising great self-control. For all the good that did. She looked at me again.

'It's dead,' she whispered. 'The bloody, blasted thing is dead ...'

In an overwhelming sense of panic, I tried the light in the hall. Zilch.

A sudden howl of wind and a clap of thunder made us both leap out of our Levis.

Susy slammed down the receiver, and shut her eyes. 'It's starting again, Arty,' she said. 'Please tell me that we've eaten Grandma Kate's poisoned cake. Please tell me that we are having halleluias.'

I hadn't even the wit to correct her. What did it matter if she used stupid words. Nor did I have the wit to remind her that we'd dumped the wretched cake. This was all for real. Another flash of lightning and rumble of thunder sent us into hysterics.

'Try the phone again,' I screeched, wishing I was old enough to have a man's voice.

'I've tried and tried,' said Susy. 'I told you, it's dead. Not a beep. What'll we do, Arty?'

What'll we do, Arty? How on earth was I supposed to know?

'Cripes, Su, we're back to spooky stuff,' I groaned. 'We didn't imagine any of it, it's as real as it could possibly be. Let's lock all the windows and doors.'

Was it really only twenty-four hours since we'd gone through all of this before? And were we to be subjected to it all again?

We went through the same ritual of locking everywhere. There was still a glimmer of daylight, but we knew it would grow dark soon. We rounded up as many candles as we could. Maybe this was just a freak storm that would pass off.

'I told you,' I cried. 'I told you we should have scarpered.'

Susy's white face turned towards me as she pressed home the latch on one of the front windows. 'Maybe he'll come anyway,' she said.

'Who? Who'll come?'

'That Garda Grogan. Maybe he'll decide to check us out anyway.'

'Fat chance,' I snorted. 'He said we were to ring if Grandma Kate didn't come back. He'll simply think that she's come back and that everything is normal. He doesn't want to be bothered with us any more. Not when he thinks we've been spinning a load of rubbishy yarns to him.'

'Oh lord!' cried Susy. 'Will we make a run for it, do you think?'

I gave a shiver at the thoughts of what might be out there lurking in the trees. If we ran out now we'd be fair game.

'Not likely,' I said. 'We'll hide in here. Come on, let's find a small place where we can lock ourselves in until this blows over.'

By now the wind had whipped up to howling pitch. The raindrops beat so hard on the window-panes that you could almost convince yourself they were fingers trying to break in. You can convince yourself of anything when hysterics hit your brain. And I tried to keep that thought to the front of my mind – that stupid hysterics were trying to do my head in and I must zap them before I went into a cringing decline.

Above all I must keep Susy from going to pieces. I had to be strong for both of us.

'Think!' I yelled at Susy. 'Where can we hide?'

Her hands were shaking as she tried to light the candles. A lighting match fell to the floor. 'Great, Susy,' I shrieked, the hysterics getting the upper hand. 'Just great. We either stay in here and be fried or else we run out and get devoured by spooks!'

Instead of being driven frantic by my outburst, Susy seemed to calm down. She stamped out the match and lit another. She held up the candle and looked at me. 'Get a grip on yourself, Arty,' she said. 'There's a small press under the worktop in the utility room.'

'The what?' I said, wishing I could get my voice down a few decibels.

'The utility room. The small room off the kitchen where Grandma Kate keeps the washing machine and things.'

'Why didn't you say so?' my words were still hitting high C. 'Come on.'

The candles flickered in the gloomy hall as we made our way down to the kitchen. When we reached it, I put my hands over my eyes so that I wouldn't look out of the window. Any sight of those flitting shadows and I'd freak out.

But I peeked. And I saw what I didn't want to see. And I freaked out.

'They're there, Susy,' I screamed. 'They're out there!'

'I don't want to know,' said Susy. She opened the door of the utility room and pushed me inside. It was small and stuffy, but its very smallness made it seem like a reasonably safe place. There was just a washing-machine, a small freezer and several presses. 'Just get in there and shut up.'

I tried to gabble something, just to show that I was in charge, but Susy grabbed me again and shoved me ahead of her into a small cupboard beside the washing-machine. A high, linen basket, half filled with laundry, took up most of the space. We squashed in behind that and blew out our candles. Then we settled back to listen to the muffled sounds of the wind and the rain and wondered would we ever leave this place.

15

We weren't there very long when we heard the first crash. Susy grabbed my arm and squeezed it. That fridge door on my neck was now permanently open and stuck with icicles.

'The studio,' I whispered. 'They're trying to get into the studio.'

'Maybe it's just the wind,' said Susy. Just then there was another tinkle of breaking glass and the rattling of a window.

Slow down, heart.

'We should have scarpered when I said,' I said bitterly. 'If we'd gone when I said, we wouldn't be here.' I couldn't see Susy, but I could feel her eyes burning in my direction.

'If we'd gone when *I* said, which was ages before you did, we wouldn't even have come back into the house at all. We'd be in the village now, eating chips in the nick and dead safe.'

'Well, here we are and here we're stuck,' I said lamely. Susy snorted. 'Maybe you're right,' I went on, trying very hard to focus my mind on real life. 'Maybe we're imagining all this. Maybe the effects of the poisoned or drugged chocolate cake is still in our system and is just giving us another bash of hallucinations.'

'Do you think so?' asked Susy. She crept closer to me and we huddled together.

'Yes,' I replied, encouraged now by having the upper hand again. 'If we concentrate very hard, we'll stop those hallucinations from taking us over. Just keep telling yourself that there's some weird stuff swimming about in your brain giving you bad vibes.'

Perhaps it was the fact that we were huddled in this safe hidey-hole that was pushing down my earlier hysteria. Also the fact that we could hardly hear the wind and rain. 'And, by the way,' I went on, 'remind me never to eat anything that Grandma Kate bakes ever again.'

The mention of Grandma Kate kind of took the good out of my logical words. Where was she? Could she really have stayed away this long just drawing? I took a deep breath, which was knocked out of me when we heard yet another crash of breaking glass.

There was no doubt this time. This was no branch, this was a serious matter of something trying to break in. All the old fears of last night came crowding back. Susy and I clutched one another, hardly daring to breathe.

'Is it people?' she whispered. 'Tell me it's just people and I'll go out there and kick their backsides. Arty? Is it people, Arty?'

I gulped. There was nothing I'd have liked better than to say it was just a bunch of thieving scumbags – in fact I'd welcome them and give them whatever they wanted, and make them tea and rustle up a rasher as well.

Another crash! Susy's nails dug into my arm. Now there were thudding sounds coming from the studio. It sounded as if they were turning the place upside down.

'They're in the...,' began Susy.

'I know, I know,' I said.

'They're smashing it up.'

'I know that too.'

'Why would they want to do that, Arty? What are they looking for?'

'How should I know?' I snapped.

'No need to take my nose off,' Susy snapped back. 'I'm only asking.'

'Sorry, Su,' I said remorsefully. No point in carrying on like this. It would get us nowhere.

'It's all to do with the studio,' I mused.

'What is?'

'All the ... the trouble. Same as last night. It all seems to stem from the studio. Think about it, Susy.'

'I'm trying to think,' she put in. 'But I'm

too scared for my brain to work.' There was a tremor in her voice.

'We *have* to try and work it out,' I hissed. 'If we just sit here and say nothing we'll go mental. We have to keep talking. Come on, think.'

I could feel Susy's warm breath in my ear as she let out a sigh. 'Okay, go on,' she said.

'The studio,' I continued. 'Why do they start there? And why was it only the studio that was messed up last night?'

'We weren't hall...imagining, were we?' whispered Susy. 'And we're not now either, are we? This has nothing to do with the chocolate cake, has it?'

I shook my head.

'Arty?' I'd forgotten she couldn't see me shaking my head.

'No,' I croaked.

'Oh cripes,' she muttered softly.

'The studio,' I went on. 'Why the studio?'

'There's nothing valuable in there,' said Susy.

'It's nothing to do with value,' I said. 'At least not money value. These...thingies would hardly be looking for something they could flog on the black market, would they?'

'Grandma Kate's paintings,' ventured Susy.

'Yeah, right. To hang in their crypts.' Was I really making a ghoulish joke at a time like this? 'Better than crawling off the wall with terror,' I said, half aloud.

'What is?' asked Susy, hoping I was going to say something very comforting, no doubt.

'Nothing,' I replied. 'And would you please lighten up your grip on my arm. Are you trying to drag the life out of me?'

As soon as I said it, something deep in the hard disc of my mind marked it as significant. But, before I could work it out, we both jumped as we heard more crashing and thumping – this time it seemed more frantic. Whatever they were after, they were desperate.

Machine-gun heart, fridge-door, crumbly bones, clammy forehead – my whole human system was breaking down. Any second now and I'd be a gibbering idiot. This time I gripped Susy's arm with one hand. The other hand was firmly clamped over my mouth to stop me from yelling out.

'Should we run for it?' whispered Susy.

'Don't be daft,' I breathed. 'How far do you think we'd get?'

'Arty,' she said nervously. 'Are they looking for us? Are they looking for you and me?'

I swallowed hard. That thought had occurred to me. But why would they want us?

'Why would they want us?' I voiced my fear.

'They didn't get what they wanted last night,' Susy went on. 'So they took Grandma Kate. Now they're back, still looking for whatever it is they want and...and...' her voice tapered off.

And if they don't find it they''ll look for us.

Neither of us said it aloud. We didn't need to. The dreadful thought was just too scary.

'Listen,' whispered Susy. We both stayed very still, not even breathing. 'It's stopped,' she went on.

Sure enough the thumping had stopped. But before we could take a breath of relief, there was a different sound. A soft, sly, hissing sound. An eerily familiar sound.

I remembered then where I'd heard that sound before.'Same sound as the bubbles in the bog,' I breathed in Susy's ear.

'Like when I threw my picture into the middle of it and it was sucked under,' she breathed back.

And then I knew! I knew the very thing that whatever was out there was looking for.

16

'That picture!' I was shaking Susy in my excitement.

'What picture?' she asked, pulling away from me. 'What are you on about?'

'The drawing that Grandma Kate was doing. The one of the tree. Where did she put it?'

'For crying out loud, Arty. What's that got to do with anything?'

'The photos of the natives!' I went on, almost incoherent with my efforts to get her to understand. I wished she could see my expression so that she'd know how sincere I was. 'You remember the natives with their faces hidden?'

'I remember. But I don't see what those photos have to do with all this. Arty, stop it. You're freaking me out. You're talking garbage. Don't do this, don't go loopy.'

'Oh Susy, think! They thought that Great-Uncle Philip was capturing their spirits in his camera....'

Susy let out a sharp breath. 'You mean...?'

'Yes! That's what I've been trying to tell you. They... these creatures think that Grandma Kate has captured their spirit in her drawing of that tree. They want that drawing. And they probably won't rest until they get it.'

'You're scaring me, Arty Adams,' said Susy. 'You've flipped. I'm out of here.' She made to get up, but I pulled her back.

'Susy!' I whispered insistently. 'You've got to listen. It makes sense. Some spooky bog creature is after the drawing. Think about it.'

Silence for a few tense moments.

'And Grandma Kate?' whispered Susy eventually. 'Will they let her go if they get it back?'

I couldn't answer that. What had they done with her? If I started to dwell on that thought. I'd definitely lose my mind. The important thing just now was to appease these creatures.

'Where did she put the picture?' I said, ignoring Susy's question. 'Can you remember?'

'She sent us up to wash our teeth,' she muttered. 'Said she was going to put her pictures in a safe place. But where? I don't know.'

'Susy,' I whispered. 'We have to find it. If we don't find it they'll come for us.'

'You mean,' she gulped. 'You mean we have to go out there and look for it? Could we not just stay here and wait it out?'

'If only we could,' I said. 'But they'd find us. We have no choice.'

'Now?' said Susy.

'Now,' I answered, wishing more than ever that we could simply bury ourselves in the laundry basket. The fact that I knew now what had to be done didn't give me any more courage. I only hoped I wouldn't fall apart before our mission was completed.

We quietly crept from our hiding-place, stretching our cramped legs in the dark of the windowless little room. With Susy holding on to my sweater, we made our way to the door.

'We've got to get across the kitchen,' I whispered. 'Not a sound, okay?' I could feel Susy's body shaking. Or was it my own?

'Arty,' Susy said softly, 'if it's a thing you're wrong about this, I'll personally cut off your head. Slowly. I'm going along with this because it seems fairly right. Just remember the head-cutting bit.'

'Thanks for that vote of confidence,' I hissed sharply. In many ways right now I wished my head *was* cut off. Then I wouldn't have to think.

The handle gave a gentle click as I turned it. We held our breath as I eased the door open. The kitchen was gloomy, but at least we could see enough not to bump into things.

The wind was still moaning outside and the rain tapped at the window. We could hear the movements in the studio, stealthy movements. They'd obviously knocked over everything and were now searching through all the drawings and canvases. I hoped they'd stay at that long enough for us to find that darn tree drawing.

We didn't dare close the door of the utility room after us in case we made noise. We tip-toed to the door leading to the hall, freezing when it creaked slightly. Susy looked fearfully towards the studio, but nothing came to investigate. Hand in hand we carried on into the hall, shivering at the sudden chill. Susy pulled my arm and pointed to the closet. I nodded and we headed towards it. There was nothing only coats and wellies. No place there to put big sketchbooks.

'There's a shelf on top,' whispered Susy. 'Lift me up and I'll rummage through it.'

With a lot of grunting, and keeping an ear cocked for any noises from the studio, I managed to raise her high enough. For a skinny little imp she weighed a ton. Must have been the new trainers. 'Hurry up,' I hissed. 'I can't hold on for longer.'

'Nothing,' she sighed, climbing down from my shoulders. 'Nothing only paint pots and gardening things. Bloody, bloody blast.'

As a sensitive and responsible lad I'd have told her to stop swearing (especially as she had a whole stock of better words than I had), but that was in the days when we'd functioned as normal people. Right now it didn't matter what words she used. In fact I was grateful for her crudeness. It helped to keep a human aspect to this bizarre scene.

'Think,' I said. 'When she told us to go and wash our teeth last night, did she follow us up or did she stay down here?'

I could see Susy's face frowning in the dim light as she tried to remember. 'I think she came up after us,' she said. 'We'd already locked up down here, so she must have come up after us. I'm pretty sure she didn't go back into the sitting-room. That door really squeaks loudly and we'd have heard it. Do you remember hearing it?'

'No.'

'I'd say she brought the sketchbook and the painting upstairs,' went on Susy.

'I hope so,' I said. Because I knew that if we went upstairs we might not get back down again to make another search. It was only a matter of time before those creatures would come looking for us.

We made our way up the stairs, dying a miserable death every time a stair creaked. We had just got as far as the landing when we heard the slithering sound down in the hall.

Susy gripped my arm. More bruises, but who was counting bruises at a time like this?

'Grandma Kate's bedroom, quickly,' I whispered in her ear. Surely that was the obvious safe place for her precious tree and hedgehog.We scrambled along the short corridor, trying to shut out the stealthy sounds from below.

Luckily there was enough light in the room for us to see fairly well. The bed was as we had left it that morning. If only we could rub out the events of the past twenty-four hours and be snuggled in there with Grandma Kate, playing pioneers in the Wild West. Except that there would have been no storm and we'd have been in our own beds. Please let me wake up in my own bed and find that all this was a nightmare. No such luck. Thank you, God. Thanks a whole bunch.

'You look under the bed,' I whispered. 'I'll try the wardrobe.'

Nothing. Not so much as a rough scribble.

'Where could she have put it?' I was getting frantic now. 'The stupid sketchbook is big enough, heaven knows. It can't be far away.'

'My room,' said Susy. 'Try my room.'

We ran back along the corridor. Susy's room was smaller than the one I was to sleep in, but it was cosier. We tried the wardrobe and the top of the wardrobe, under the bed, in the chest of drawers. Nothing. We'd just pulled out a big roll of canvas when we heard the stairs creak.

Ssss...sss... There was no mistaking that sound. And there was no mistaking where it was headed.

17

I tried to take a deep breath, but the air wouldn't go all the way to the bottom of my lungs. I felt like I was drowning in fear.

Sss... sss... slither. They were on their way up here. For us.

'Jump out of the window, Arty!' cried Susy.

It was tempting, but one of us would twist an ankle or break a leg. Anyway, I knew that Grandma Kate's life depended on us getting that sketch to these creatures. There was only one more room to try.

'My room!' I said. 'It must be there.'

A flash of inspired memory reminded me that my bedroom was used as a kind of boxroom where Grandma Kate stored things. How well Susy had been given the cosy room! But this wasn't the time for the peeved grandson act. We ran across the floor, all efforts at stealth now no longer necessary – those spooks knew we were here anyway. Susy was ahead of me when we hit the corridor.. She skidded to a halt, her breath wiped away in a sharp gasp.

In the gloomy light we could see a thick layer of slime oozing in our direction, cutting off the stairs and cutting off the route to my room. Bits of twigs and branches, like bony, grasping fingers, brushed against the wallpaper on either side of the narrow corridor. Here and there bigger masses of the stuff rose above the level of the rest, masses that, though shapeless, seemed to be leading the creeping terror. I just hoped they wouldn't emerge from their muddy cover.

The smell of rotting vegetation once again pushed its way into our nostrils, making us gag.

'Arty!' screamed Susy, turning back and clutching my sweater.

We shrank back from the mass of slime and vegetation that was flowing towards us. A quick decision had to be made. I gripped Susy's hand.

'We have to run for it,' I cried. 'We have to get to my room. That drawing has to be in there. Don't let go of my hand. No matter what, don't let go.'

I could feel her nails biting into my hand. I tried to take another deep breath, but the rancid air stopped at my throat. With a last squeeze on Susy's hand, I pulled her into the river of boggy ooze. At first our feet skipped over the surface, steering clear of the shapeless mounds that dripped and bent towards us. But the farther we got the heavier and stickier it became. We could hear the slurp as we pulled our feet clear.

'Get off!'

I turned to see what Susy was shouting at and felt a panicky stab in my stomach when I saw a root-like strand wind itself around her legs.

'Hold on!' I shouted.

I pulled and pulled at her hand, but I could feel her slipping. 'Grab my sweater,' I sobbed. 'Susy, don't let go!'

With a pitiful cry, she lost her grip and was dragged from my grasp. I tried to reach back for her, but by now there were several roots wrapping themselves around my ankles. They were pulling me down into the boggy slime.

Was this to be the end of Susy and Grandma Kate and me? And all for a stupid old drawing? I should bloomin' well think not! A vision of Great-uncle Philip in Africa flashed to my mind. A bunch of upset natives didn't deter him, so why should I be scared of a load of soggy turf? With a terrifying battle-cry – well, a bit of a croak actually – I tore at the branches. I was so surprised when I broke free that I almost stood long enough to let them grab me again.

Do I go for Susy, or do I get the drawing?

Think, Arty. I picked the drawing.

'Please, please let it be in my room,' I gasped, pulling my feet clear with a grim, determined effort. By now, of course, my boots were back somewhere in the slurping mess. Roots shot out to grab at me, but I soldiered on. I could hear Susy crying out and using some of her choice words. At least she was still alive.

'Hold on, Susy!' I shouted. 'Don't let them pull you under.'

I flung open the door of my room. The oozing mess surged along after me. I had only the barest seconds before I'd be submerged. Mercifully the light had become brighter by now. Was it dawn already?

A quick glance around the room. In one corner stood a sort of trestle table and, on it, a bundle of sketchbooks and canvases. I dashed across and began to rummage. Pictures of every sort of creature and flower, but no tree. I threw them on the floor in frustration. If the tree had been put here it would have been on top.

My breath was coming out in short gasps. The oozing mass was at my feet. The tendrils were reaching out, looking more like spooky hands than ever. And I knew that those shapeless masses were about to reveal themselves. And I knew that when they did, I'd freak out and all would be lost.

As I turned away to pull my feet free, my eye caught a portfolio leaning against the wall beside my bed. With a superhuman pull, I got one foot clear. It was just enough to allow me to reach for the portfolio. My fingers were almost there. Another inch. The pull on my foot was stronger. There were awful noises behind me. Almost human. Those masses were about to become creatures so terrible I'd die. My strength was giving way now.

'Arty!' Susy's muffled cry gave me one last spurt of energy.

I scrabbled at the portfolio until it fell towards me. Hardly conscious of the fact that the branches had my legs and feet firmly in their grasp, I tore it open. And there it was, in all its awful glory.

The tree!

'I have it!' I cried. 'I have what you want! Here, take it. Take your spirit away with you.'

I held the drawing towards the mass of now heaving shapes. What seemed like a bony branch shot out from one of the shapes and took the drawing. It touched me briefly on the index finger of my left hand. A slimy, damp touch. With a slurp, the drawing disappeared into the middle of the undulating mass.

Suddenly my feet were free as the tide of boggy matter retreated out the door. I ran after it and watched in amazement as it withdrew quickly along the corridor and down the stairs. No tracks were left. No slime of vegetation to show what had been here. The wind died down and the rain stopped beating on the windows. Silence.

'Well, would you look at that!'

Susy! She was sitting outside Grandma Kate's bedroom. 'Would you just look at that,' she said again. I ran to her .

'Susy, you're okay!' I shouted.

'I am in me eye,' she muttered, pointing to her feet. 'Look what those stupid mudballs did to my new trainers! And they cost me a ruddy fortune,' she added, reaching down and trying to wipe the mud off. 'I've a good mind to...what are you laughing at, Arty Adams?'

18

We collapsed on the sofa in the sitting-room, totally exhausted. Neither of us wanted to talk. What could we possibly say to one another? Words would just seem so pointless after what we'd just been through. The early morning sun shone through the window, making a big yellow rectangle on the carpet. There were no tracks, no slime and no bits of vegetation left in any part of the house. Except for our stained clothes, including Susy's peaty trainers of course, there was no evidence of our visitors from the bog.

'What now?' Susy asked eventually. 'What do we do next, Arty?'

I didn't know. I didn't even want to think. I just wanted to sit here and let that warm sun wash over me. But I knew Susy was right. We'd have to work up the energy to go and look for Grandma Kate. I tried not to dwell on the possibility that she might not be found.

'Arty? What do we do now?'

'Just give me a minute to get my head

together,' I said, letting my legs flop over the arm of the sofa. 'I'm so t...'

'Ssshhh,' Susy sat up straight, her head cocked.

I swung around to face her. 'What?'

She put her finger to her lips. And then I heard it too. It was the stealthy sound of someone trying the front door. All the blood drained from my body and would have run out of my feet if I didn't have my socks on. Now we could hear movement around the side of the house. Whoever, or whatever, was out there was going around to the back door.

'Not again,' I groaned softly. 'I can't take any more of this, Susy. What more can we do? What could they possibly want now?'

Susy's white face was tense and tired. 'Us?' she whispered. 'I'll just die, Arty.'

We jumped, clutching one another tightly when the kitchen door opened.

I was about to shout 'Run!' as a sudden surge of self-preservation hit me, when a voice called out from the hall, 'Hello.'

Marsh monsters don't say hello, I thought. Do they?

'It's Grandma Kate!' shouted Susy. 'Oh, Arty, it's Grandma Kate!'

She leapt off the sofa as our granny peered into the sitting-room. Her ponytail had come undone and her hair hung limply around her grubby face. Her clothes were grubby too and very creased. She closed her eyes with relief as she hugged the two of us very tightly. We had begun to babble all together when another figure loomed in the doorway.

'Mr Kitt,' said Grandma Kate, easing herself up. 'Come down to the kitchen and we'll all have a cup of tea.'

Mr Kitt was as filthy as Grandma Kate. The peat dust had settled in the lines on his forehead and in the stubble on his face, making him look like a drawing where someone had gone too heavily with the pencil. He sat slumped at the kitchen table, his expression flashed between puzzlement, fear and relief. His hand shook as Susy handed him a cup of steaming hot tea. She and I had figured we were in the best shape to make the breakfast. The toast I'd made lay untouched. Nobody felt like eating, even though I'd carefully scraped away the burnt bits.

Susy was jigging up and down in her chair, like she normally does when she's dying to ask a question.

'What happened to you, Mr Kitt?' She couldn't hold back any longer.

Mr Kitt shook his head slowly. 'I honestly don't know,' he said. 'One minute I was going over to my truck. Just after I'd been talking to...to your granny.' He looked sheepishly at Grandma Kate as if remembering the painful conversation they'd been having. 'Next thing I know she's hauling me out of a bog-hole and, well, here I am.'

I nudged Susy so that she wouldn't blab on about spooks and all that. He hadn't mentioned them, so he mustn't have seen them. I should have given her more credit. She narrowed her eyes at me and mouthed, 'I'm not a fool.'

'Lucky I was out early,' put in Grandma Kate. 'Or you might still be there. Dangerous things, bog-holes.'

So, he thought she'd just come along this morning. Now I wondered if she herself remembered anything that happened to her. But I couldn't ask, not yet.

'You've said it, missus,' agreed Mr Kitt. 'I must have hit my head when I fell. I feel like I've been knocked out for days.'

'You have,' said Susy gleefully. 'It's a whole day and two nights since we were talking to you.'

Mr Kitt's eyes opened wide. 'Good grief!' he exclaimed. 'That long!'

'Isn't it a wonder your sister didn't have the gardai out looking for you,' Susy added, with a gleam of mischief in her eyes.

Mr Kitt looked surprised for a moment,

then he nodded. 'Ah, Tess is used to me coming and going,' he said. 'I do be away on business a lot.'

'I'll bet,' whispered Susy, close to my ear. I smothered a giggle.

Mr Kitt turned to Grandma Kate again. 'I'm very glad you came along,' he went on. 'That place is dangerous. I had no idea.'

'Well,' I put in with, I must admit, a hint of malice, 'when you bring in your heavy machinery you'll be able to ...'

'What!' he looked at me with horror. 'I wouldn't touch that place with a barge-pole. Not if it was the last place on earth. No,' he said to Grandma Kate, 'you're welcome to that part of the bog, missus. It will always give me the creeps. You can have it.'

'Is it for the animals?' asked Susy. 'Are you leaving it alone for the sake of the animals and the plants?'

Mr Kitt snorted. 'Not so much that,' he said. 'It's them bog-holes. If anyone working in the bog fell into one of them bog-holes like I did, they'd sue me.'

Money, I thought. After all that, he was still concerned about money. Some things don't change.

Grandma Kate tried to hide her grin by taking a sip of her now cold tea. 'Will you be all right?' she asked, as Mr Kitt got up to leave. 'Will I run you home in my car?'

'I'll be fine,' he said. 'The Land Rover's still in the bog. I'll get home and clean up. Thanks again.'

We watched him shuffle off through the long grass towards the bog – Grandma Kate's bog.

'And now,' said Grandma Kate. 'Tell me what went on here, you two.'

Sitting on the warm step outside the front door, we told her everything. Now and then she'd throw her hands up in horror and hug us hard. 'Oh my poor dears,' she'd mutter. 'It's too much. It's all just too much.'

When we came to the bit about the bog creatures wanting the drawing back, she was gobsmacked. She looked at me in amazement. 'How did you know, Arty? How did you know that was what they wanted?'

'The photos you'd been showing us,' I said. 'The old photos the Great-uncle Philip took, remember? You told us about the natives who thought that the camera would suck out their spirits.'

Realisation dawned on her and she looked at me with total respect.

'And you worked out, from that story, that the bog wanted its spirits back? The spirits in that old tree I was sketching. The spirits of the bog! Good heavens. I knew, all the time

I'd been working on that tree, there was something very special about it. Which is why I opted to do a picture of it, I suppose.'

'Well, you'd better stick to bunnies and blossoms, Gran,' said Susy.

Grandma Kate laughed and ruffled Susy's hair.

'What about you?' I asked. 'Do you remember what happened to you?'

She gazed out into the distance. 'Do I remember?' she mused. 'I'll remember it for the rest of my life.' She looked first at Susy and then at me. 'All I could think of as I was dragged off was would you two be all right. I was so worried about you that I hardly had time to think about what was happening...'

'Get on to the dragging away bit,' put in Susy.

Grandma Kate looked into the distance again. 'When I came downstairs,' she went on, 'I suddenly felt my feet go from under me. I thought one of you had left something in the hall. Before I had time to call out, I was covered by this soft, cold stuff. It was pitch dark, but I knew there was some kind a presence there, in all that slime. I could feel someone or something watching me. I knew then that it wasn't thieves I was up against. I cried out several times, asking what did they want. I pleaded with them to let me go, that I meant them no harm, so why did they want to do me harm?'

'And did they answer?' I asked.

'No,' she replied. 'All I could hear was a hissing sound. Sss...sss... It was scary, I can tell you.'

'We sure as hell know that,' muttered Susy.

'Of course you do,' said Grandma Kate, not even giving out to Susy for being so rude. 'I feel so bad about what you've both been through.'

'What happened next?' I asked.

Grandma Kate shrugged her shoulders. 'That's it,' she said.

'That's it!' echoed Susy. 'What happened when you got to the bog?'

'I don't know. All I remember is crying out to whoever it was to tell me what they wanted. Then, next thing I knew, I came to this morning in a bog-hole at the foot of that big tree. Mr Kitt was half-buried a short distance away. I fished him out. He thought he'd simply stumbled into a bog-hole, so I let him go on believing that, even though I knew something very strange had happened.'

'Just as well,' I said. 'He'd blab that story all over the place. Sell it to some sleazy paper and you'd have gangs of people traipsing out here.'

Grandma Kate shook her head. 'Perish the

thought,' she said with a laugh. 'As it is he just thinks the place is full of bog-holes, so he won't want anyone around. That suits me and my wildlife just fine.'

'The bog creatures must have known what he was up to,' said Susy. 'They must have sensed that he meant to cut up that part of the bog. The part with the old tree.'

'So the bog decided to zap him,' I put in. 'Cool.'

'Well, no. We wouldn't wish that on him,' smiled Grandma Kate. 'Anyway, there's no danger to that little haven now. Heavens, if only I'd known.'

'Known what?' I asked.

'If only I'd known they were after that drawing it would have saved so much scary stuff for you two.'

Susy looked at me and we both grinned a special grin which can only be shared by people who've been part of a living nightmare.

'What do you say to a visit to the cinema tonight?' asked Grandma Kate. 'This holiday starts right now, okay?'

'Now you're talking my language,' said Susy.

There was a soft snuffling sound in the undergrowth. The three of us laughed when Hoggy the hedgehog emerged. But when he saw that it was still daylight, he retreated into the thick cover of long grass and poppies.

'What does he want?' said Grandma Kate. 'Hedgehogs only come out at night.'

'Except when they're having their portraits done,' laughed Susy.

'That's it,' I said. 'He wants his spirit back!'

I neatly dodged the kick from Susy's bog-stained trainer.